新制多益聽力題庫

會話大全❶

TOEIC

Amanda Chou ◎ 著

四大特色

1 填空題設計：逐步聽懂細節訊息和掌握關鍵字彙

納入對話填空題設計，挖空部分均為官方必考話題，同步掌握細節訊息和相關專業字彙。

2 獨立對話題演練：搭配詳盡解析，一次搞懂所有出題考點

精選試題，並加入完整解析，確實掌握出題者思維和慣用語表達，胸有成竹的應對新制題型。

3 獨立對話模擬試題練習：熟悉此長度的對話練習

藉由對話模擬試題演練，漸進式養成具備獨立撰寫此長度的聽力內容，並能獨自演練完整一回的聽力試題。

4 更廣的題材納入：提升學習興趣和強化答題靈活度

收錄更多元的對話題材和道地慣用語，從演練有趣話題中拓展思路，提升臨場答題反應力。

作者序

聽力的養成其實需要一段時間，而對於初、中階的學習者，更需要紮實、循序漸進的訓練才能有所成效。

首先練習書中part 1的對話題庫中填空和拼字練習，降低聽一個對話寫試題所造成的難度。將目標先放在：聽對話時要求自己完成挖空的常見字彙並記憶這些常見字彙。在每個part 1中的空格都能拚對字彙時，開始練習聽力專注力，藉由part 1的46則對話練習「影子跟讀」，修正聽力專注力和回想剛才對話內容，有助於學習者逐步掌握主旨或70%的內容。有了這樣的基礎後，再來答新多益的對話，就能發揮練習越多題目越能漸漸掌握出題和擴充自己的聽力語彙等能力，且不會有挫折感產生。

再來可以開始進一步規劃part 2的部分。在part 2則以新多益單一一篇的對話搭配詳盡的解析，考生練習習題，在透過解析的輔助，補強自己不足的部分，外加每篇對話均為中英對照，更便於考生閱讀。寫完試題後，更能重複檢視考點和練習影子跟讀，強化自己的聽力實力。

最後的一個階段是part 3的部分。在這部分考生可以練習「一整回」對話模擬試題的演練（即連續寫13篇對話一氣呵成），如果可以很輕易達到這個目標的時候，考生就能開始大量寫一整回的聽力模擬試題練習了（即包含part1-4的練習）。

規劃本書希望能協助考生累積實力，並逐步完成聽一整回新多益會話的模擬試題（每回包含13個對話），且不費吹灰之力獨立完成撰寫模擬試題題庫，對答案備考，中間不會有太多的停頓以及挫折感。根據這本新多益會話大全的規劃且反覆聆聽書中的試題和音檔，逐步達到這個目標。

Amanda Chou

使用說明

INSTRUCTIONS

Unit 12 安裝電話費用的紛爭

UNIT ⓬

安裝電話費用的紛爭

▶「短對話」填空練習 MP3 012

除了前面的**「影子跟讀短對話練習」**，現在試著在聽完對話後，完成下列對話中填空部分，從中強化生活場景中常見的字彙以及拼字能力，答案的話請參照前面的對話喔！

Mark: How is your ________ going?	**馬克**：你的家用電話都裝好了嗎？
Jennifer: It is going ok, but I received ________ asking for the ________, and I remembered clearly there is no ________.	**珍妮佛**：還好，可是我收到一張帳單說要收安裝費，我記得很清楚你說過沒有安裝費的。
Mark: There is no installation fee, if you are switching from another phone ________, but for the new client there is an ________.	**馬克**：如果你有安裝過別家公司的電話，那是沒有安裝費的。可是如果是全新用戶那就會有。
Jennifer: Well, that is not what I was told. I would not have ________ with you if I knew, there is going to be an installation charge. What ________ do I have to sign to ________ the service?	**珍妮佛**：可是我聽到的不是這樣，我如果知道有安裝費用我就不會選擇你們公司。那我要取消，要填什麼表格呢？
Mark: I am sorry you are under the ________, let me check with my boss and see what I can do.	**馬克**：不好意思你可能誤會我的意思，讓我問一下我的上司看能怎麼處理。
Jennifer: Now you are talking, I am sure you don't want to lose a ________.	**珍妮佛**：這才對，你一定也不想失去一個客戶。

060 061

基礎實力養成，完成所有填空題
聽力細節的掌握能力也同步飆升

- 先藉由填空題演練，掌握字彙部分，再延伸學習到聆聽一整篇對話，大幅降低挫折感，增進學習動力。
- 掌握必考商業和生活字彙並反覆練習，直至所有規劃的填空練習均能聽對，再進行聽一段對話並完成試題的練習。

「影子跟讀」強化聽力耳
聽力專注力立馬到位，答題不失分

- 由「中英對照」的對話以影子跟讀法進行練習，從「看原稿跟著音檔讀」逐步延伸至「只播放音檔也能同步跟著讀」等等的練習，打好聽力專注力基礎。並於具備一定的聽力專注力後再輔以海量的試題搭配練習，分數迅速狂飆。

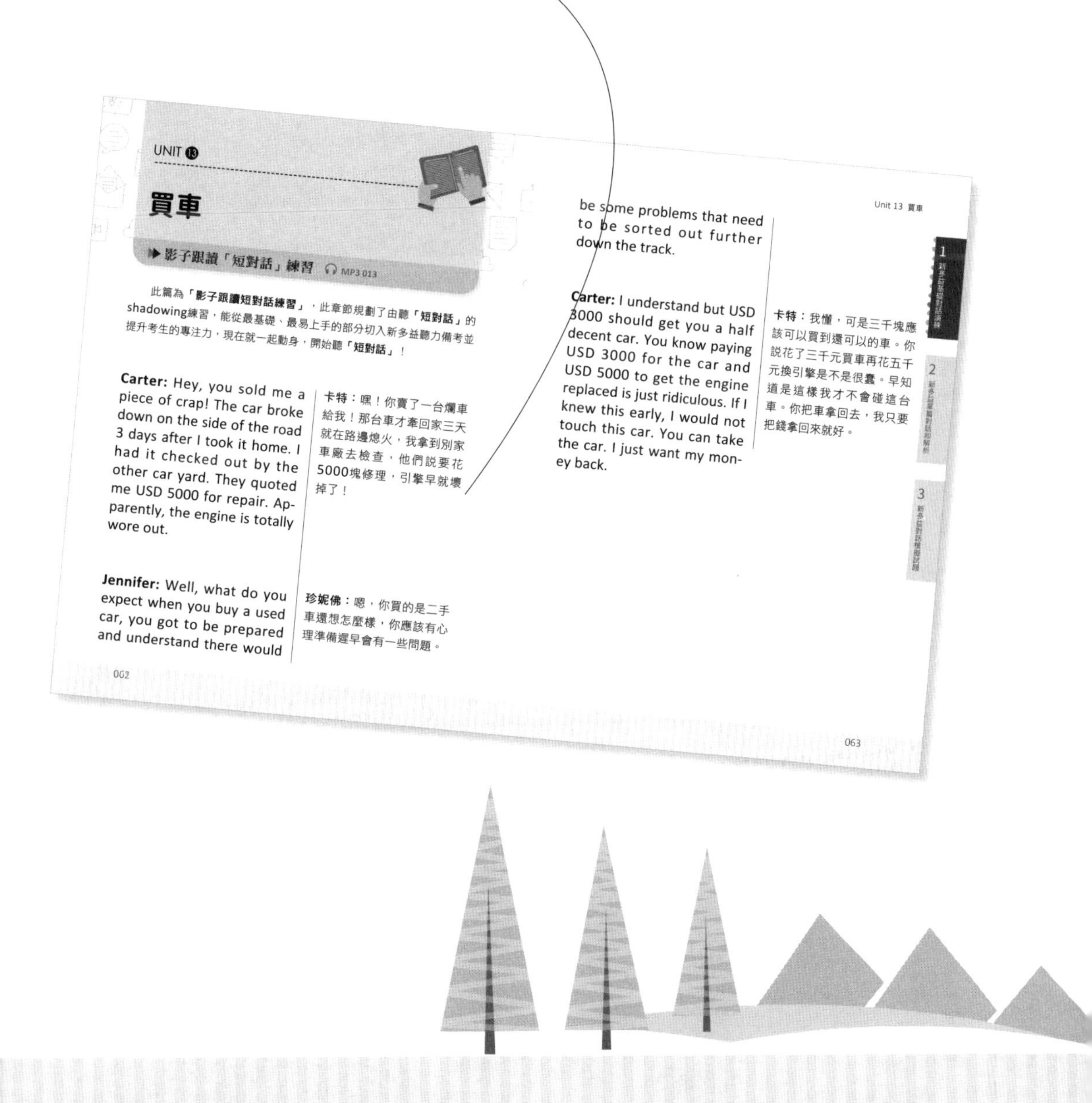

UNIT 13

買車

▶影子跟讀「短對話」練習 MP3 013

此篇為「**影子跟讀短對話練習**」，此章節規劃了由聽「**短對話**」的shadowing練習，能從最基礎、最易上手的部分切入新多益聽力備考並提升考生的專注力，現在就一起動身，開始聽「**短對話**」！

Carter: Hey, you sold me a piece of crap! The car broke down on the side of the road 3 days after I took it home. I had it checked out by the other car yard. They quoted me USD 5000 for repair. Apparently, the engine is totally wore out.

卡特：嘿！你賣了一台爛車給我！那台車才牽回家三天就在路邊熄火，我拿到別家車廠去檢查，他們說要花5000塊修理，引擎早就壞掉了！

Jennifer: Well, what do you expect when you buy a used car, you got to be prepared and understand there would be some problems that need to be sorted out further down the track.

珍妮佛：嗯，你買的是二手車還想怎麼樣，你應該有心理準備遲早會有一些問題。

Carter: I understand but USD 3000 should get you a half decent car. You know paying USD 3000 for the car and USD 5000 to get the engine replaced is just ridiculous. If I knew this early, I would not touch this car. You can take the car. I just want my money back.

卡特：我懂，可是三千塊應該可以買到還可以的車。你說花了三千元買車再花五千元換引擎是不是很囊。早知道是這樣我才不會碰這台車。你把車拿回去，我只要把錢拿回來就好。

062

Unit 13 買車

063

中英對照設計
便於考生觀看和練習

・撰寫一篇英文對話練習並對答案與觀看解析後，重複檢視考點並進行影子跟讀練習，再次強化聽力弱項和漏聽的部分，完善備考練習，於正式考試時，不再錯相同考點或漏聽相似句，穩守得分。

Unit 1

停車場看出職場地位

Instructions

❶ 請播放音檔聽下列對話，並完成試題。MP3 047

1. What are the three people talking about?
(A) how to walk to the parking lot
(B) walking a lot is good for health
(C) the reason that they need to park far away from the building
(D) the reason that someone in a higher position parks farther from the building

2. Why do they need to park at D lot?
(A) because D lot is closer to the company
(B) because they are assistants
(C) because they want to walk a lot
(D) because it is free to park at D lot

3. Why does the man say, "I'm feeling a little better"?
(A) because those in higher positions also need to walk the same distance to the parking lot as he does
(B) because he feels walking to the parking lot makes him more energetic
(C) because he enjoys the conversation with the woman
(D) because those in higher positions decided to give him a promotion

198

Unit 1 停車場看出職場地位

中譯與聽力原文

Questions 1-3 refer to the following conversation

James: Why do we have to park at D lot? It's five blocks away from the entrance building.
詹姆士：為什麼我們要停在D停車場呢？離建築物入口要走五個街區。

Mary: Assistants park at D lot. That's the rule, unless you get promoted.
瑪　莉：助理停在D停車場。這是規定，除非你獲得升遷。

James: Right, managers can park at B lot, two blocks away, and of course CEOs and clients, A lot.
詹姆士：是啊，經理能停在B停車場，距離兩個街區遠，然後當然CEO和客戶停在A停車場。

Linda: You know what...what makes me feel better is that C lot and D lot are all five blocks away from the building, but
琳　達：你知道嗎？...使我感到好多了的是C停車場和D停車場同樣都離建築物五個街區，

199

1 新多益各種對話演練
2 新多益單篇對話和解析
3 新多益對話模擬試題

Jim: It's like life. Life is like a box of chocolates; you don't know what it is until you experience it.

吉姆： 就像生命一樣。人生像是一盒巧克力，你不知道會是什麼直到你體驗了。

選項中譯與解析

19. 他們在談論什麼節日？
(A) 聖誕節。
(B) 感恩節。
(C) 情人節。
(D) 復活節。

20. 說話者對花束和巧克力看法如何？
(A) 難過的。
(B) 挫折的。
(C) 開心的。
(D) 不確定的。

21. 「人生像是一盒巧克力」，這句話含意為何？
(A) 我們無法預測我們會發生什麼事。
(B) 我們應該多吃巧克力。
(C) 巧克力有益健康。
(D) 生活苦樂參半，就像巧克力一樣。

19.
．聽到對話，馬上鎖定關鍵字Valentine's Day，可知對話談論的是情人節。配合對話gets a bouquet and a box of chocolate等內容，最符合情人節的送禮項目，故此題**答案為C**。此題屬於情境題，可以直接鎖定對話關鍵字Valentine's Day，接著透過對話中的bouquet、a box of chocolate和gets a boutique from an admirer等細節來驗證，最符合這樣的節日就是情人節，所以答案即為C。

20.
．根據對話，How sweet is that、makes my day、so fancy等感嘆語和形容詞，可知收到花束和巧克力是讓人感到十分貼心和雀躍的。此題屬於細節題及推測題，考生須先理解慣用語make one's day的意思，接著推測與make one's day相關的情緒形容詞。片語make one's day有讓人非常開心的意思，就像讓人的一天都因此而美好，搭配對話中提到的sweet、fancy，都有很正向的意思，所以與其最相近的就是選項**(C)cheerful快樂的**。

21.
．需特別留意結論句you don't know what it is until you experience it.由此可知，人生像一盒巧克力，是因為必須品嚐了才知道滋味，故此題**答案為A**。此題屬於推測題，考生須根據題目細節推測答案，可以搭配選項的刪去法來解答。Life is like a box of chocolate，是比喻的句型。又根據對話關鍵句：you don't know what it is until you experience it「必須經歷才能理解」來對照選項，可知選項A的內容「人生是無法預測的」和題目意義最為相近。也可先刪除錯誤的B、C選項；而**D選項「人生有苦有甜」是一個誘答選項要特別小心**。

1 新多益基礎對話演練
2 新多益單篇對話和解析
3 新多益對話模擬試題

附選項中譯和詳盡解析
徹底理解所有出題脈絡

．提供更多元的答題思路，逐步協助考生進行推論或刪去誘答選項，釐清頭緒後迅速判答，如同有英文家教在旁的神力加持，自觀自學即可完成所有試題並具備應考判答實力。

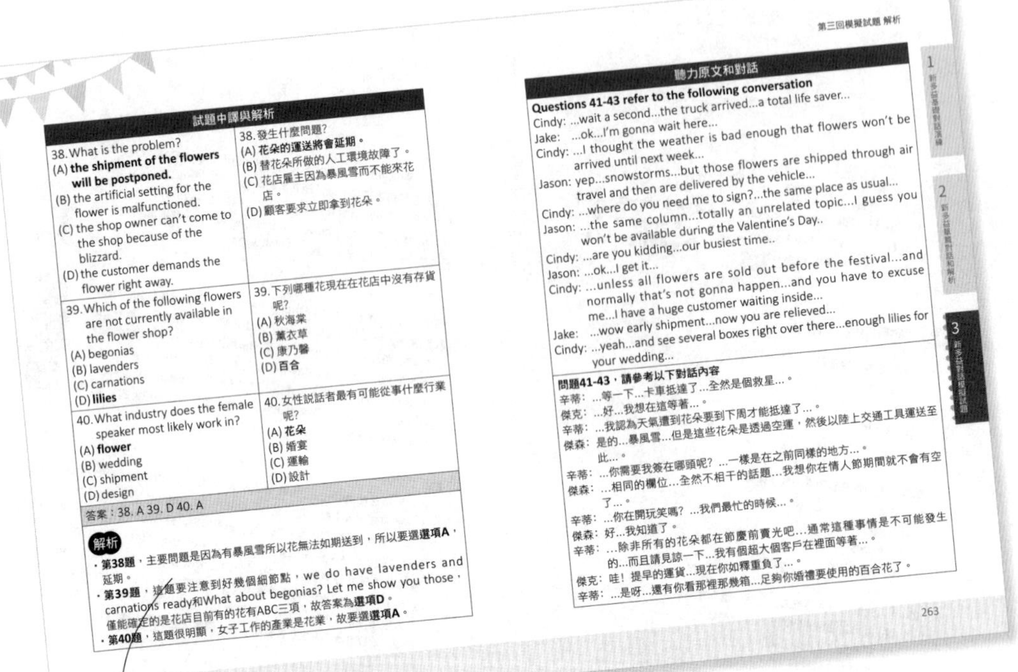

第三回模擬試題 解析

試題中譯與解析

38. What is the problem? (A) **the shipment of the flowers will be postponed.** (B) the artificial setting for the flower is malfunctioned. (C) the shop owner can't come to the shop because of the blizzard. (D) the customer demands the flower right away.	38. 發生什麼問題? (A) **花朵的運送將會延期。** (B) 替花朵所做的人工環境故障了。 (C) 花店雇主因為暴風雪而不能來花店。 (D) 顧客要求立即拿到花朵。
39. Which of the following flowers are not currently available in the flower shop? (A) begonias (B) lavenders (C) carnations (D) **lilies**	39. 下列哪種花現在在花店中沒有存貨呢? (A) 秋海棠 (B) 薰衣草 (C) 康乃馨 (D) **百合**
40. What industry does the female speaker most likely work in? (A) **flower** (B) wedding (C) shipment (D) design	40. 女性說話者最有可能從事什麼行業呢? (A) **花朵** (B) 婚宴 (C) 運輸 (D) 設計

答案：38. A 39. D 40. A

解析

- **第38題**，主要問題是因為有暴風雪所以花無法如期送到，所以要選**選項A**，延期。
- **第39題**，這題要注意到好幾個細節點，we do have lavenders and carnations ready和What about begonias? Let me show you those，僅能確定的是花店目前有的花有ABC三項，故答案為**選項D**。
- **第40題**，這題很明顯，女子工作的產業是花業，故要選**選項A**。

262

聽力原文和對話

Questions 41-43 refer to the following conversation

Cindy: ...wait a second...the truck arrived...a total life saver...
Jake: ...ok...I'm gonna wait here...
Cindy: ...I thought the weather is bad enough that flowers won't be arrived until next week...
Jason: yep...snowstorms...but those flowers are shipped through air travel and then are delivered by the vehicle...
Cindy: ...where do you need me to sign?...the same place as usual...
Jason: ...the same column...totally an unrelated topic...I guess you won't be available during the Valentine's Day..
Cindy: ...are you kidding...our busiest time..
Jason: ...ok...I get it...
Cindy: ...unless all flowers are sold out before the festival...and normally that's not gonna happen...and you have to excuse me...I have a huge customer waiting inside...
Jake: ...wow early shipment...now you are relieved...
Cindy: ...yeah...and see several boxes right over there...enough lilies for your wedding...

問題41-43，請參考以下對話內容

辛蒂：...等一下...卡車抵達了...全然是個救星...。
傑克：...好...我想在這等著...。
辛蒂：...我認為天氣遭到花朵要到下周才能抵達了...。
傑森：是的...暴風雪...但是這些花朵是透過空運，然後以陸上交通工具運送至此...。
辛蒂：...你需要我簽在哪頭呢? ...一樣是在之前同樣的地方...。
傑森：...相同的欄位...全然不相干的話題...我想你在情人節期間就不會有空了...。
辛蒂：...你在開玩笑嗎? ...我們最忙的時候...。
傑森：好...我知道了。
辛蒂：...除非所有的花朵都在節慶前賣光吧...通常這種事情是不可能發生的...而且請見諒一下...我有個超大個客戶在裡面等著...。
傑克：哇！提早的運貨...現在你如釋重負了...。
辛蒂：...是呀...還有你看那裡那幾箱...足夠你婚禮要使用的百合花了。

263

1 新多益基礎對話演練
2 新多益單篇對話和解析
3 新多益對話模擬試題

演練 13 篇為一組的英文對話
適應應考時英文對話節奏

- 習慣性聽此長度的英文對話，立即熟悉一整回聽力模擬試題中對話練習量（即 13 篇），漸進式養成具備獨立撰寫聽力試題的實力。
- 搭配所附的中英對照和解析，雙重檢視學習成果，一舉攻略新多益聽力。

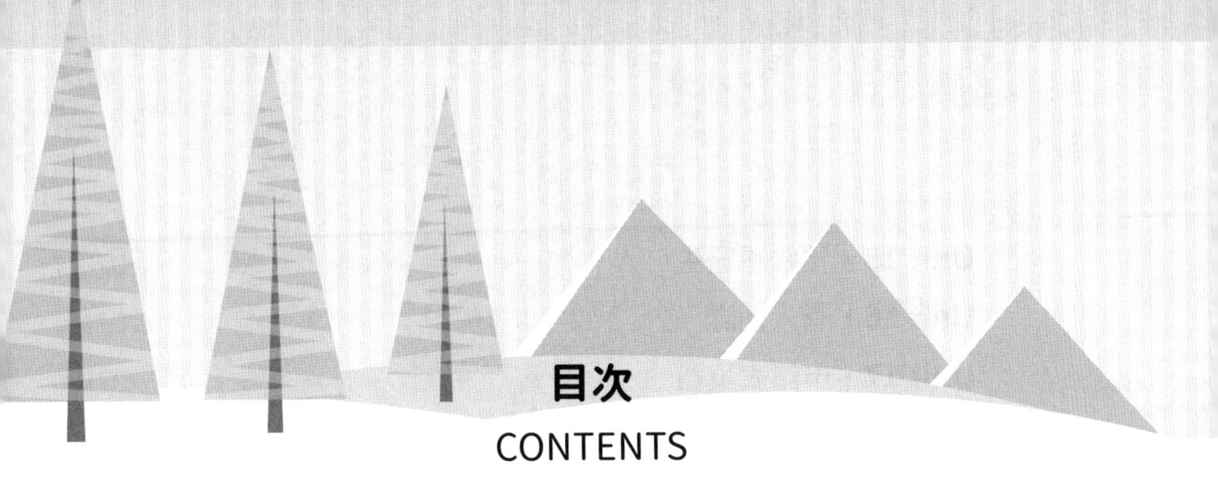

目次

CONTENTS

Part 1 新多益基礎對話演練

Part 2 新多益單篇對話和解析

Part 3 新多益對話模擬試題

簡短對話

- 【倍斯特空服：説謊話】
  可別拿紅酒來滅火啊！
- 【倍斯特空服：模擬機艙】
  什麼？...我不會拿到負面的評論了吧！
- 【倍斯特花店】
  我們確實備有室內耕種的薰衣草和康乃馨
- 【倍斯特花店】
  花朵提早運至真的如釋重負了
- 【倍斯特跨國海產公司】
  居然一下就錄取了，可是有這麼容易嗎？

- 【倍斯特跨國海產公司】

  跟當初說的全然不同，去拿午餐盒吧（唉）！

- 【倍斯特跨國海產公司】

  招聘手冊和網站介紹原來在騙人啊！

- 【倍斯特水族館：談價格】

  議價沒這麼容易，不過確實還有很多細節要談

- 【倍斯特水族館：見面勘場】

  勘場的驚喜，水族館有個城堡啊！

- 【倍斯特旅行社】

  駱駝騎乘服

- 【倍斯特手錶】

  居然送了手錶仿冒品，有安全疑慮時還真的輕忽不得

- 【倍斯特傢俱行】

  傢俱訂購，公司客服一一搞定後續延伸問

- 【倍斯特銀行】

  銀行交易出現異常，不會是駭客吧！

UNIT 1

機場接機

▶▶影子跟讀「短對話」練習 MP3 001

此篇為**「影子跟讀短對話練習」**，此章節規劃了由聽**「短對話」**的shadowing練習，能從最基礎、最易上手的部分切入新多益聽力備考並提升考生的專注力，現在就一起動身，開始聽**「短對話」**！

Customer service: I am afraid all our drivers are flat out at the moment. I would suggest you take a taxi from the airport to the campus, but it would cost you an arm and a leg.

客服：很抱歉我們司機現在都很忙。我建議您自己搭計程車到學校，可是車費會很貴。

Mark: Would you refund the cost of the pickup service since I was not picked up?

馬克：那你會退我接機的費用嗎？畢竟沒有人來接我啊。

Customer service: Unfortu-

客服：恐怕不行，因為接機

nately, it has all been pre-paid, and it is customer's responsibility to provide us the correct flight details.

服務都是預付的，而且提供正確的行程表是客人的責任。

Mark: That is totally unfair! I did provide the correct itinerary to my agent. It is not my fault if the information somehow got lost in the system. I can't get hold of my agent due to the time difference. If I would be charged anyway, I would rather stick around here for your next available driver.

馬克：這真是太不公平了，我有通知代辦中心我更改了機位，你們沒有收到正確的訂位紀錄不是我的錯。因為時差的關係我聯絡不上代辦中心。如果你們堅持要收費的話，那我情願等你們的司機有空。

UNIT ❶

機場接機

▶▶「短對話」填空練習 MP3 001

除了前面的**「影子跟讀短對話練習」**，現在試著在聽完對話後，完成下列對話中填空部分，從中強化生活場景中常見的字彙以及拼字能力，答案的話請參照前面的對話喔！

Customer service: I am afraid all our ________ are flat out at the ________. I would suggest you take a ________ from the ________ to the ________, but it would cost you an ________ and a leg.	**客服：**很抱歉我們司機現在都很忙。我建議您自己搭計程車到學校，可是車費會很貴。
Mark: Would you ________ the cost of the ________ since I was not picked up?	**馬克：**那你會退我接機的費用嗎？畢竟沒有人來接我啊。
Customer service: Unfortu-	**客服：**恐怕不行，因為接機

nately, it has all been ______ ____, and it is customer's ____ ______ to provide us the correct ________.

服務都是預付的，而且提供正確的行程表是客人的責任。

Mark: That is totally unfair! I did provide the correct ____ ______ to my ________. It is not my fault if the ________ somehow got lost in the ____ _____. I can't get hold of my agent due to the ________. If I would be ________ anyway, I would rather stick around here for your next available driver.

馬克：這真是太不公平了，我有通知代辦中心我更改了機位，你們沒有收到正確的訂位紀錄不是我的錯。因為時差的關係我聯絡不上代辦中心。如果你們堅持要收費的話，那我情願等你們的司機有空。

UNIT ❷

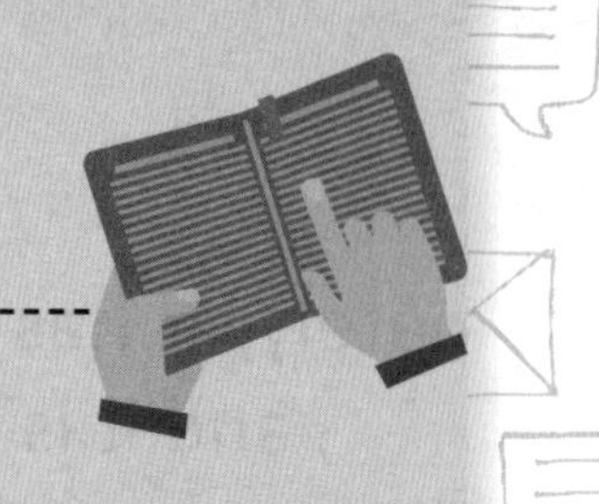

註冊費遲交

▶▶影子跟讀「短對話」練習 MP3 002

此篇為**「影子跟讀短對話練習」**，此章節規劃了由聽**「短對話」**的shadowing練習，能從最基礎、最易上手的部分切入新多益聽力備考並提升考生的專注力，現在就一起動身，開始聽**「短對話」**！

Mark: Hi, I received this letter stating I have to pay an additional 200 dollars for the delayed student fee.

馬克：您好，我收到這封信説我的註冊費遲繳，要多交200美金的遲交罰金。

Sally: Well, you got that right! The tuition was late by 2 days. Unfortunately, if you wish to avoid the late fee, you got to be in time.

收銀員莎莉：你説對了，你的學費晚了兩天入帳。很遺憾地，如果你不想被罰錢的話，就要及時繳交。

Mark: That is unreasonable. You've got to understand I

馬克：這不合理，你要知道我是留學生，我的學費是從

am an international student and my fees are wire transferred directly into the school account from overseas. My parents definitely did it before the deadline; however, we have no control of when the money would reach the school account. I can show you the bank receipt as the proof of payment it was done before the deadline. I think it should be sufficient enough for the late fees to be waived.

國外直接電匯到學校的帳戶。我爸媽真的是在期限前去電匯的，只是我們無法控制要花多長的時間錢才會入帳。我有銀行水單可以做憑證，學費是在期限前匯的。這樣應該可以免去遲繳罰金了吧！

UNIT ❷

註冊費遲交

▶▶「短對話」填空練習 MP3 002

除了前面的**「影子跟讀短對話練習」**，現在試著在聽完對話後，完成下列對話中填空部分，從中強化生活場景中常見的字彙以及拼字能力，答案的話請參照前面的對話喔！

Mark: Hi, I received this ____ ______ stating I have to pay an _________ dollars for the delayed _________.	**馬克：**您好，我收到這封信說我的註冊費遲繳，要多交200美金的遲交罰金。
Sally: Well, you got that right! The _________ was late by 2 days. Unfortunately, if you wish to avoid _________, you got to be in time.	**收銀員莎莉：**你說對了，你的學費晚了兩天入帳。很遺憾地，如果你不想被罰錢的話，就要及時繳交。
Mark: That is _________. You've got to understand I	**馬克：**這不合理，你要知道我是留學生，我的學費是從

am an ________ student and my ________ are wire transferred ________ into the ________ from overseas. My parents definitely did it before the ________; however, we have no control of when the ________ would reach the school account. I can show you the ________ as the proof of ________ it was done before the deadline. I think it should be ________ enough for the late fees to be ________.

國外直接電匯到學校的帳戶。我爸媽真的是在期限前去電匯的，只是我們無法控制要花多長的時間錢才會入帳。我有銀行水單可以做憑證，學費是在期限前匯的。這樣應該可以免去遲繳罰金了吧！

UNIT 3

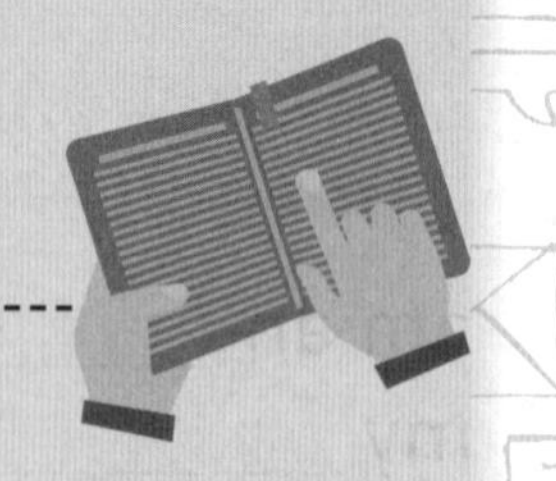

選課錯誤

▶▶ 影子跟讀「短對話」練習 MP3 003

此篇為**「影子跟讀短對話練習」**，此章節規劃了由聽**「短對話」**的shadowing練習，能從最基礎、最易上手的部分切入新多益聽力備考並提升考生的專注力，現在就一起動身，開始聽**「短對話」**！

Mary: I am sorry that I screwed this up, how could I not have realized Marketing 101 is the pre-requisite for Advance Marketing? I have pulled out from Advance Marketing, but all the Marketing 101 classes are full.

瑪莉：我很抱歉我搞砸了，我怎麼會不知道行銷學 101 是進階行銷學的基礎課程。我已經取消進階行銷學的選課了，可是行銷學 101 的課全是滿的。

Mr. Larson: This happens every semester. It was mentioned over and over, but no one pays any attention on what we said. Unfortunately,

拉森先生：這種事怎麼每個學期都發生，我們說了又說可是都沒有人聽進去。很可惜地目前我幫不上你忙，最好的方式就是等開學後有人

there is nothing I can do at this moment, your best bet would be waiting for someone to drop this unit and hopefully you can take over the spot. Otherwise, you would have to wait for next semester then.

要退選，希望你可以填上那個空缺，不然你就只好等下學期了。

Mary: Please do your best to squeeze me in; otherwise, I would have to put off graduation for another 6 months.

瑪莉：求求你盡力把我排進去，不然我要延六個月才能畢業。

UNIT 3

選課錯誤

▶▶「短對話」填空練習 MP3 003

除了前面的**「影子跟讀短對話練習」**，現在試著在聽完對話後，完成下列對話中填空部分，從中強化生活場景中常見的字彙以及拼字能力，答案的話請參照前面的對話喔！

Mary: I am sorry that I ______ ____ this up, how could I not have realized Marketing 101 is the __________ for Advance Marketing? I have pulled out from Advance Marketing, but all the Marketing 101 ______ ____ are full.

瑪莉：我很抱歉我搞砸了，我怎麼會不知道行銷學 101 是進階行銷學的基礎課程。我已經取消進階行銷學的選課了，可是行銷學 101 的課全是滿的。

Mr. Larson: This happens every __________. It was mentioned over and over, but no one pays any __________ on what we said. Unfortunately,

拉森先生：這種事怎麼每個學期都發生，我們說了又說可是都沒有人聽進去。很可惜地目前我幫不上你忙，最好的方式就是等開學後有人

there is nothing I can do at this moment, your best bet would be waiting for someone to ________ this unit and hopefully you can take over the ________. Otherwise, you would have to wait for ________ then.

要退選，希望你可以填上那個空缺，不然你就只好等下學期了。

Mary: Please do your best to ________; otherwise, I would have to put off ________ for another ________.

瑪莉：求求你盡力把我排進去，不然我要延六個月才能畢業。

UNIT 4

銀行開戶

▶▶ 影子跟讀「短對話」練習 MP3 004

此篇為**「影子跟讀短對話練習」**，此章節規劃了由聽**「短對話」**的shadowing練習，能從最基礎、最易上手的部分切入新多益聽力備考並提升考生的專注力，現在就一起動身，開始聽**「短對話」**！

Mark: I know what you are saying, but I was told all I need is the letter from the university to prove I am a student which entitles me to open a student account. I was not aware I also need to bring a proof of address as well.

馬克：我知道你的意思，可是有人跟我說我只需要大學出的證明信函說我是學生，這樣我就可以開一個學生帳戶。我不知道我還需要地址證明。

Mary Ann: Well, because you are an overseas student, we need to verify the documents carefully. Do you have any-

瑪麗安：嗯，因為你是國際學生，所以我們需要小心地審核所有文件，你可以提出你住在學校宿舍的證明嗎？

thing which can prove you will be staying in the university dormitory?

Mark: I only arrived in the country last night. All I have is a receipt to prove I paid for the accommodation for this semester. If this wasn't sufficient, I really don't know what to do. Would you consider calling the university to verify my address? Tell me what else I can do.

馬克：我昨天才抵達，我只有一張宿舍繳費的收據，證明繳了一學期。如果這樣無法接受的話，那我不知道要怎麼辦。或是你可以直接打電話給我的學校，跟他們確認我的地址，這是我唯一想到的辦法。

UNIT 4

銀行開戶

▶▶「短對話」填空練習 MP3 004

除了前面的**「影子跟讀短對話練習」**，現在試著在聽完對話後，完成下列對話中填空部分，從中強化生活場景中常見的字彙以及拼字能力，答案的話請參照前面的對話喔！

Mark: I know what you are saying, but I was told all I need is the ________ from the ________ to prove I am a student which entitles me to open a student ________. I was not aware I also need to bring a proof of ________ as well.

馬克：我知道你的意思，可是有人跟我說我只需要大學出的證明信函說我是學生，這樣我就可以開一個學生帳戶。我不知道我還需要地址證明。

Mary Ann: Well, because you are an ________ student, we need to ________ the ________ carefully. Do you have

瑪麗安：嗯，因為你是國際學生，所以我們需要小心地審核所有文件，你可以提出你住在學校宿舍的證明嗎？

anything which can prove you will be staying in the university ________?

Mark: I only arrived in the ________ last night. All I have is a ________ to prove I paid for the ________ for this ________. If this wasn't sufficient, I really don't know what to do. Would you ________ calling the university to verify my address? Tell me what else I can do.

馬克：我昨天才抵達，我只有一張宿舍繳費的收據，證明繳了一學期。如果這樣無法接受的話，那我不知道要怎麼辦。或是你可以直接打電話給我的學校，跟他們確認我的地址，這是我唯一想到的辦法。

UNIT 5

作業要求延遲交件

▶▶ 影子跟讀「短對話」練習 MP3 005

此篇為**「影子跟讀短對話練習」**，此章節規劃了由聽**「短對話」**的shadowing練習，能從最基礎、最易上手的部分切入新多益聽力備考並提升考生的專注力，現在就一起動身，開始聽**「短對話」**！

Jerry: I know you don't like to hear about this, but I am here to ask for the deferral for the final assignment. All I am asking is just one extra week.

傑瑞：我知道你聽到這個一定不高興，但是我不得已要來跟您要求期末作業需要延期交件，只要給我多一個星期就好。

Professor Lin: Reason being?

林教授：是什麼原因？

Jerry: My parents made it clear that I have to be able to support myself even if I am a full time student. I work my

傑瑞：我爸媽明確的要求我一定要自力更生，就算我是全職的學生也是一樣。我很努力地兼了兩份差還要當全

ass off juggling between two part-time jobs and a full time study. You've got to give me some credit for it.

職的學生，這樣應該算是正當理由吧！

Professor Lin: That's not my problem. You should have planned it better.

林教授：那不是我的問題，你應該更有效率的安排你的時間。

Jerry: I am enrolled in 3 units this semester and how they schedule the assignments is out of my hands. All of the assignments are due in the same week. I just need some extra help.

傑瑞：我這學期選了三門課，我沒有辦法控制老師要怎麼安排交作業的時間表，所有的作業都需要在同一個星期交件，我只是需要多一點幫助。

UNIT 5

作業要求延遲交件

▶▶「短對話」填空練習 MP3 005

除了前面的**「影子跟讀短對話練習」**，現在試著在聽完對話後，完成下列對話中填空部分，從中強化生活場景中常見的字彙以及拼字能力，答案的話請參照前面的對話喔！

Jerry: I know you don't like to ________ about this, but I am here to ask for the ____ ____ for the final ________. All I am asking is just one extra week.	**傑瑞**：我知道你聽到這個一定不高興，但是我不得已要來跟您要求期末作業需要延期交件，只要給我多一個星期就好。
Professor Lin: ________ being?	**林教授**：是什麼原因？
Jerry: My ________ made it clear that I have to be able to ________ myself even if I am	**傑瑞**：我爸媽明確的要求我一定要自力更生，就算我是全職的學生也是一樣。我很

a full time student. I work my ass off ________ between two part-time jobs and a ________ study. You've got to give me some ________ for it.

努力地兼了兩份差還要當全職的學生，這樣應該算是正當理由吧！

Professor Lin: That's not my problem. You should have ________ it better.

林教授：那不是我的問題，你應該更有效率的安排你的時間。

Jerry: I am enrolled in ________ this semester and how they ________ the assignments is out of my hands. All of the assignments are due in the same week. I just need some ________.

傑瑞：我這學期選了三門課，我沒有辦法控制老師要怎麼安排交作業的時間表，所有的作業都需要在同一個星期交件，我只是需要多一點幫助。

UNIT 6

科目被當見教授

▶▶ 影子跟讀「短對話」練習 MP3 006

此篇為**「影子跟讀短對話練習」**，此章節規劃了由聽**「短對話」**的shadowing練習，能從最基礎、最易上手的部分切入新多益聽力備考並提升考生的專注力，現在就一起動身，開始聽**「短對話」**！

Zoe: Hi, Professor Hopkins, I am here to have a chat about my result.	**若儀：**您好，霍普金斯教授，我想來跟您談談我的成績。
Professor Hopkins: Let me bring up your record. Well, you are two marks short for passing which is a shame.	**霍普金斯教授：**讓我調你的資料出來看一下。嗯，你其實差兩分就可及格，真可惜。
Zoe: I wondered whether it is possible for me to redo my mid-term paper to see if I can make up for those two	**若儀：**我想問問看是不是可以讓我重做我的期中作業，看看我是不是可以多得到我需要的兩分，你可以查查看

marks that I need. You can check my attendance, I never missed a single lecture, and I got 30 out of 40 in my final.

我的出席率，我從來沒有缺課，我的期末考也有 75 分。

Professor Hopkins: Well, considering you did quite well in your final exam. I would go out of my way to help you. I will give you a week. Come and see me next Wednesday and I will go through your paper again.

霍普金斯教授：這麼說來你的期末考還考得不錯，我特別幫你一個忙，給你一個禮拜，下星期三帶作業來給我看看。

UNIT 6

科目被當見教授

「短對話」填空練習 MP3 006

除了前面的**「影子跟讀短對話練習」**，現在試著在聽完對話後，完成下列對話中填空部分，從中強化生活場景中常見的字彙以及拼字能力，答案的話請參照前面的對話喔！

Zoe: Hi, Professor Hopkins, I am here to have a ________ about my ________.	**若儀**：您好，霍普金斯教授，我想來跟您談談我的成績。
Professor Hopkins: Let me bring up your record. Well, you are two marks short for passing which is a shame.	**霍普金斯教授**：讓我調你的資料出來看一下。嗯，你其實差兩分就可及格，真可惜。
Zoe: I wondered whether it is ________ for me to redo my ________ to see if I can make up for those ________	**若儀**：我想問問看是不是可以讓我重做我的期中作業，看看我是不是可以多得到我需要的兩分，你可以查查看

that I need. You can check my _________, I never missed a single _________, and I got 30 out of _________ in my final.

我的出席率，我從來沒有缺課，我的期末考也有 75 分。

Professor Hopkins: Well, considering you did quite well in your final exam. I would go out of my way to help you. I will give you ___________. Come and see me next _________ and I will go through your paper again.

霍普金斯教授：這麼說來你的期末考還考得不錯，我特別幫你一個忙，給你一個禮拜，下星期三帶作業來給我看看。

UNIT 7

買學生票沒帶證件

▶▶影子跟讀「短對話」練習 MP3 007

此篇為**「影子跟讀短對話練習」**，此章節規劃了由聽**「短對話」**的shadowing練習，能從最基礎、最易上手的部分切入新多益聽力備考並提升考生的專注力，現在就一起動身，開始聽**「短對話」**！

Mark: Oh no! I just realized I left my student ID in the dorm. Can I still get a student ticket?

馬克：喔糟糕！我剛剛才發現我的學生證丟在宿舍裡。我還可以買學生票嗎？

Kimberly: I am sorry. I have to verify the ID before I can sell you the student ticket.

金柏莉：很抱歉我必須看過你的證件才可以賣學生票給你。

Mark: I know I should have my student ID to be able to be entitled to a student discount. Let me see what else I

馬克：我知道我必須要有學生證才可以享有學生折扣，讓我看看我還有什麼，我剛好有一份作業，上面的日期

got. I actually have a copy of my assignment, which dated last week. I think it should be good enough to prove I am currently enrolled. Come on, I know you can make the final call.

是上星期。這應該足以證明我是在學學生了吧！別這樣嘛，我知道你有權力決定。

Kimberly: Well, I suppose I can look the other way. That's good enough for me.

金柏莉：嗯，我看我就網開一面好了，這樣就足以證明了。

Mark: Thanks heaps! You are the best! I am sure no one goes this far to scam the system.

馬克：太感謝你了，你真是個好人！ 我知道應該沒有人會為了騙一張學生票而做到這種程度的吧！

UNIT 7

買學生票沒帶證件

▶▶「短對話」填空練習 MP3 007

除了前面的**「影子跟讀短對話練習」**，現在試著在聽完對話後，完成下列對話中填空部分，從中強化生活場景中常見的字彙以及拼字能力，答案的話請參照前面的對話喔！

Mark: Oh no! I just realized I left my ________ in the ____ _____. Can I still get a _____ ___?	**馬克：**喔糟糕！我剛剛才發現我的學生證丟在宿舍裡。我還可以買學生票嗎？
Kimberly: I am sorry. I have to verify the ID before I can sell you the student ticket.	**金柏莉：**很抱歉我必須看過你的證件才可以賣學生票給你。
Mark: I know I should have my student ID to be able to be entitled to a student ____ _____. Let me see what else I	**馬克：**我知道我必須要有學生證才可以享有學生折扣，讓我看看我還有什麼，我剛好有一份作業，上面的日期

got. I actually have a __________ of my assignment, which dated __________. I think it should be good enough to prove I am __________ enrolled. Come on, I know you can make the final call.

是上星期。這應該足以證明我是在學學生了吧！別這樣嘛，我知道你有權力決定。

Kimberly: Well, I suppose I can look the other way. That's good enough for me.

金柏莉：嗯，我看我就網開一面好了，這樣就足以證明了。

Mark: Thanks heaps! You are the best! I am sure no one goes this far to __________ the system.

馬克：太感謝你了，你真是個好人！ 我知道應該沒有人會為了騙一張學生票而做到這種程度的吧！

UNIT 8

宿舍室友吵鬧

▶▶影子跟讀「短對話」練習 MP3 008

此篇為**「影子跟讀短對話練習」**，此章節規劃了由聽**「短對話」**的shadowing練習，能從最基礎、最易上手的部分切入新多益聽力備考並提升考生的專注力，現在就一起動身，開始聽**「短對話」**！

Mary: hey, I know you are probably still hangover, but I really need to speak to you about something. It has been bothering me for a long time.

瑪莉：我知道你可能還在宿醉，可是我真的忍無可忍了，一定要跟你說，我已經忍耐很久了。

Cameron: What is it？

卡麥倫：到底什麼事？

Mary: I've had enough of the chatting, and the loud music every night. All I want to do is have a good night sleep, I've got to go to work in the

瑪莉：我真的受不了你每天晚上又是聊天又是吵鬧的音樂，我真的只想睡個好覺，你要知道我早上要上班，下午還要上課。

morning and classes in the afternoon.

Cameron: I am sorry but you can join us if you want.

卡麥倫：不好意思啦！你也可以加入我們啊！

Mary: I don't want to join you, and I am not telling you what not to do, but every night of the week is just too much to handle. I can tolerate it on the weekends, but please, not the week nights.

瑪莉：我不想加入你們！我也不是教你都不要這樣，只是一個禮拜七天都這樣真的太過分了。如果只是週末我還可以忍受，可是拜託，一到五不要好不好。

UNIT 8

宿舍室友吵鬧

「短對話」填空練習 MP3 008

除了前面的**「影子跟讀短對話練習」**，現在試著在聽完對話後，完成下列對話中填空部分，從中強化生活場景中常見的字彙以及拼字能力，答案的話請參照前面的對話喔！

Mary: hey, I know you are probably still ________, but I really need to speak to you about something. It has been ________ me for a long time.	**瑪莉：**我知道你可能還在宿醉，可是我真的忍無可忍了，一定要跟你說，我已經忍耐很久了。
Cameron: What is it？	**卡麥倫：**到底什麼事？
Mary: I've had enough of the ________, and the ________ every night. All I want to do is have a good night ____	**瑪莉：**我真的受不了你每天晚上又是聊天又是吵鬧的音樂，我真的只想睡個好覺，你要知道我早上要上班，下

______, I've got to go to work in the morning and classes in the ________.

午還要上課。

Cameron: I am sorry but you can join us if you want.

卡麥倫：不好意思啦！你也可以加入我們啊！

Mary: I don't want to join you, and I am not telling you what ________, but every night of the week is just too much to ________. I can ________ it on the weekends, but please, not the week nights.

瑪莉：我不想加入你們！我也不是教你都不要這樣，只是一個禮拜七天都這樣真的太過分了。如果只是週末我還可以忍受，可是拜託，一到五不要好不好。

UNIT 9

共同廚房誰整理

▶▶影子跟讀「短對話」練習 MP3 009

此篇為**「影子跟讀短對話練習」**，此章節規劃了由聽**「短對話」**的shadowing練習，能從最基礎、最易上手的部分切入新多益聽力備考並提升考生的專注力，現在就一起動身，開始聽**「短對話」**！

Tracey: Hey Stephen, can I ask you to clean up the dishes once you are done cooking? Just in case you didn't notice. I have been cleaning up after you for more than a week now.

崔西：嘿，史蒂芬，我可以麻煩你在煮完飯之後把碗洗一洗嗎？你可能沒有注意到，這一個禮拜多來都是我在幫你洗碗。

Stephen: Oh.. Did I not do that? Ok..

史蒂芬：喔…我真的沒有洗嗎？ 那...好...。

Tracey: I am not trying to be a pain in the ass, but I am

崔西：我不是想要找你麻煩，可是我真的受不了一直

just sick of tidying up for others. I got lots of studies to catch up. I don't mind helping you out once a while, if you got caught up with things, but not all the time.	幫人收拾善後。我自己有很多書要讀，如果你忙的話，我不介意偶爾幫一次，可是不能每次都指望我。
Stephen: I am sorry I didn't realise I haven't been doing it. I guess my mind was somewhere else.	**史蒂芬：**真的很抱歉，我一直沒注意到我都沒做，可能我都在想別的事。
Tracey: That's all right, I am not trying to make you feel bad, I just want to draw your attention to it.	**崔西：**沒關係，我不是想讓你覺得難堪，我只是想讓你注意到這件事。

UNIT 9

共同廚房誰整理

▶▶「短對話」填空練習 MP3 009

除了前面的**「影子跟讀短對話練習」**，現在試著在聽完對話後，完成下列對話中填空部分，從中強化生活場景中常見的字彙以及拼字能力，答案的話請參照前面的對話喔！

Tracey: Hey Stephen, can I ask you to clean up the ____ ______ once you are done cooking? Just in case you didn't __________. I have been __________ up after you for more than a week now.	**崔西：**嘿，史蒂芬，我可以麻煩你在煮完飯之後把碗洗一洗嗎？你可能沒有注意到，這一個禮拜多來都是我在幫你洗碗。
Stephen: Oh.. Did I not do that? Ok..	**史蒂芬：**喔…我真的沒有洗嗎？那...好...。
Tracey: I am not trying to be a pain in the ass, but I am	**崔西：**我不是想要找你麻煩，可是我真的受不了一直

just sick of __________ up for others. I got lots of __________ to catch up. I don't __________ helping you out once a while, if you got caught up with things, but not all the time.

幫人收拾善後。我自己有很多書要讀，如果你忙的話，我不介意偶爾幫一次，可是不能每次都指望我。

Stephen: I am sorry I didn't realise I haven't been doing it. I guess my __________ was somewhere else.

史蒂芬：真的很抱歉，我一直沒注意到我都沒做，可能我都在想別的事。

Tracey: That's all right, I am not trying to make you __________, I just want to draw your __________ to it.

崔西：沒關係，我不是想讓你覺得難堪，我只是想讓你注意到這件事。

UNIT ⑩

房屋修繕

▶▶影子跟讀「短對話」練習 MP3 010

此篇為**「影子跟讀短對話練習」**，此章節規劃了由聽**「短對話」**的shadowing練習，能從最基礎、最易上手的部分切入新多益聽力備考並提升考生的專注力，現在就一起動身，開始聽**「短對話」**！

Peter: Hello Mrs. Moore. I came to see you today because I reported the problem of the leaking tap in my bathroom last month, and you promised me the plumber would be here in a few days, but till now he is nowhere to be seen still.

彼得：摩爾先生您好，我今天來是因為我上個月就跟你説過浴室的水龍頭在漏水。你答應我水電工這幾天就會來，可是一直都沒有人來修。

Mrs. Moore: Oh... my apologies. I will get onto it on Monday.

摩爾太太：不好意思，我星期一會馬上辦。

Peter: Do you realize how much we have to pay for our last water bill? It cost 50 dollars extra! I am only a student, and I don't make a lot of money and I hope you are willing to cover the extra cost until the tap is fixed. If the plumber did not show up on Monday, I would hire one to fix it myself and send the bill to you.

彼得：你知道我們上個月的水費繳多少錢嗎？比平常多 50 美金。我只是個學生，賺的錢不多，我希望在水龍頭修好之前你要負擔額外的水費。如果水電工星期一再不來修，我只好自己請人來修然後把帳單寄給你。

UNIT ⑩

房屋修繕

▶▶「短對話」填空練習 MP3 010

除了前面的「**影子跟讀短對話練習**」，現在試著在聽完對話後，完成下列對話中填空部分，從中強化生活場景中常見的字彙以及拼字能力，答案的話請參照前面的對話喔！

Peter: Hello Mrs. Moore. I came to see you ________ because I ________ the problem of the leaking tap in my ________ last month, and you promised me the ________ would be here in ________, but till now he is nowhere to be seen still.

彼得：摩爾先生您好，我今天來是因為我上個月就跟你說過浴室的水龍頭在漏水。你答應我水電工這幾天就會來，可是一直都沒有人來修。

Mrs. Moore: Oh... my ________. I will get onto it on ________.

摩爾太太：不好意思，我星期一會馬上辦。

Peter: Do you realize how much we have to pay for our last __________? It cost 50 dollars extra! I am only a __________, and I don't make a lot of money and I hope you are willing to cover the extra cost until the tap __________. If the plumber did not show up on __________, I would __________ one to fix it myself and send the __________ to you.

彼得：你知道我們上個月的水費繳多少錢嗎？比平常多 50 美金。我只是個學生，賺的錢不多，我希望在水龍頭修好之前你要負擔額外的水費。如果水電工星期一再不來修，我只好自己請人來修然後把帳單寄給你。

UNIT ⓫

退租押金

▶▶影子跟讀「短對話」練習 MP3 011

此篇為**「影子跟讀短對話練習」**，此章節規劃了由聽**「短對話」**的shadowing練習，能從最基礎、最易上手的部分切入新多益聽力備考並提升考生的專注力，現在就一起動身，開始聽**「短對話」**！

Mr. Ferguson: I am happy with the general condition of the wall and the carpet, but the kitchen cabinet doors need to be replaced. The condition is appalling. I would have to deduct USD 150 from your bond.

佛格森先生：這房子的牆面及地毯大概的情況都還好，可是廚房儲物櫃的門需要更換，怎麼會弄得這麼糟？我必須扣你150美金的押金。

Claire: I do apologize. My boyfriend thought the door was jammed and he pulled it too hard. The hinges just came off. I think you can eas-

克萊兒：真的很抱歉，我男朋友以為櫥櫃門卡住了就用力拉，誰知道太用力了，櫃子的樞軸就掉下來了。我覺得如果找個雜工來處理應該

ily repair it if you get a handyman in. It would not cost USD 150, would it? I think USD 100 would be a fair price. I mean the condition of the cabinet door was not too flash when we moved in to start with. You can see for yourself we do try to take a good care of this place.

很容易更換，這應該不需要150 美金吧！100 應該就可以了吧！因為我們搬進來的時候櫥櫃門本來就有點舊，你應該也看的出來我們一直都很照顧這個房子。

UNIT ⓫

退租押金

▶▶「短對話」填空練習 MP3 011

除了前面的**「影子跟讀短對話練習」**，現在試著在聽完對話後，完成下列對話中填空部分，從中強化生活場景中常見的字彙以及拼字能力，答案的話請參照前面的對話喔！

Mr. Ferguson: I am happy with the __________ of the __________ and the __________, but the__________ doors need to be replaced. The condition is __________. I would have to __________ USD 150 from your __________.

佛格森先生：這房子的牆面及地毯大概的情況都還好，可是廚房儲物櫃的門需要更換，怎麼會弄得這麼糟？我必須扣你 150美金的押金。

Claire: I do apologize. My boyfriend thought __________ was jammed and he pulled it too hard. The __________ just came off. I think you can eas-

克萊兒：真的很抱歉，我男朋友以為櫥櫃門卡住了就用力拉，誰知道太用力了，櫃子的樞軸就掉下來了。我覺得如果找個雜工來處理應該

ily repair it if you get a handyman in. It would not cost USD 150, would it? I think USD 100 would be a fair price. I mean the condition of the cabinet door was not too flash when we moved in to start with. You can see for ________ we do try to take a good care of ________.

很容易更換，這應該不需要 150 美金吧！100 應該就可以了吧！因為我們搬進來的時候櫥櫃門本來就有點舊，你應該也看的出來我們一直都很照顧這個房子。

UNIT ⑫

安裝電話費用的紛爭

▶▶影子跟讀「短對話」練習 MP3 012

此篇為**「影子跟讀短對話練習」**，此章節規劃了由聽**「短對話」**的shadowing練習，能從最基礎、最易上手的部分切入新多益聽力備考並提升考生的專注力，現在就一起動身，開始聽**「短對話」**！

Mark: How is your home phone going?	**馬克：**你的家用電話都裝好了嗎？
Jennifer: It is going ok, but I received the bill asking for the installation fee, and I remembered clearly there is no installation fee.	**珍妮佛：**還好，可是我收到一張帳單說要收安裝費，我記得很清楚你說過沒有安裝費的。
Mark: There is no installation fee, if you are switching from another phone company, but for the new client there is an	**馬克：**如果你有安裝過別家公司的電話，那是沒有安裝費的。可是如果是全新用戶那就會有。

installation charge.

Jennifer: Well, that is not what I was told. I would not have signed up with you if I knew, there is going to be an installation charge. What form do I have to sign to cancel the service?

珍妮佛：可是我聽到的不是這樣，我如果知道有安裝費用我就不會選擇你們公司。那我要取消，要填什麼表格呢？

Mark: I am sorry you are under the wrong impression, let me check with my boss and see what I can do.

馬克：不好意思你可能誤會我的意思，讓我問一下我的上司看能怎麼處理。

Jennifer: Now you are talking, I am sure you don't want to lose a customer

珍妮佛：這才對，你一定也不想失去一個客戶。

UNIT 12

安裝電話費用的紛爭

▶▶「短對話」填空練習 MP3 012

除了前面的**「影子跟讀短對話練習」**，現在試著在聽完對話後，完成下列對話中填空部分，從中強化生活場景中常見的字彙以及拼字能力，答案的話請參照前面的對話喔！

Mark: How is your ________ going?	**馬克：**你的家用電話都裝好了嗎？
Jennifer: It is going ok, but I received ________ asking for the ________, and I remembered clearly there is no ________.	**珍妮佛：**還好，可是我收到一張帳單說要收安裝費，我記得很清楚你說過沒有安裝費的。
Mark: There is no installation fee, if you are switching from another phone ________, but for the new client there	**馬克：**如果你有安裝過別家公司的電話，那是沒有安裝費的。可是如果是全新用戶那就會有。

is an ________.

Jennifer: Well, that is not what I was told. I would not have ________ with you if I knew, there is going to be an installation charge. What ________ do I have to sign to ________ the service?

珍妮佛：可是我聽到的不是這樣，我如果知道有安裝費用我就不會選擇你們公司。那我要取消，要填什麼表格呢？

Mark: I am sorry you are under the________, let me check with my boss and see what I can do.

馬克：不好意思你可能誤會我的意思，讓我問一下我的上司看能怎麼處理。

Jennifer: Now you are talking, I am sure you don't want to lose a ________.

珍妮佛：這才對，你一定也不想失去一個客戶。

UNIT ⓭

買車

▶▶影子跟讀「短對話」練習 MP3 013

此篇為**「影子跟讀短對話練習」**，此章節規劃了由聽**「短對話」**的shadowing練習，能從最基礎、最易上手的部分切入新多益聽力備考並提升考生的專注力，現在就一起動身，開始聽**「短對話」**！

Carter: Hey, you sold me a piece of crap! The car broke down on the side of the road 3 days after I took it home. I had it checked out by the other car yard. They quoted me USD 5000 for repair. Apparently, the engine is totally wore out.

卡特：嘿！你賣了一台爛車給我！那台車才牽回家三天就在路邊熄火，我拿到別家車廠去檢查，他們說要花5000塊修理，引擎早就壞掉了！

Jennifer: Well, what do you expect when you buy a used car, you got to be prepared and understand there would

珍妮佛：嗯，你買的是二手車還想怎麼樣，你應該有心理準備遲早會有一些問題。

be some problems that need to be sorted out further down the track.

Carter: I understand but USD 3000 should get you a half decent car. You know paying USD 3000 for the car and USD 5000 to get the engine replaced is just ridiculous. If I knew this early, I would not touch this car. You can take the car. I just want my money back.

卡特：我懂，可是三千塊應該可以買到還可以的車。你說花了三千元買車再花五千元換引擎是不是很蠢。早知道是這樣我才不會碰這台車。你把車拿回去，我只要把錢拿回來就好。

UNIT 13

買車

▶▶「短對話」填空練習 MP3 013

除了前面的**「影子跟讀短對話練習」**，現在試著在聽完對話後，完成下列對話中填空部分，從中強化生活場景中常見的字彙以及拼字能力，答案的話請參照前面的對話喔！

Carter: Hey, you sold me a piece of ________! The car broke down on the side of the road ________ after I took it home. I had it checked out by the other car yard. They quoted me USD 5000 for ________. Apparently, the ________ is totally wore out.

卡特：嘿！你賣了一台爛車給我！那台車才牽回家三天就在路邊熄火，我拿到別家車廠去檢查，他們說要花5000塊修理，引擎早就壞掉了！

Jennifer: Well, what do you ________ when you buy a ________, you got to be pre-

珍妮佛：嗯，你買的是二手車還想怎麼樣，你應該有心理準備遲早會有一些問題。

pared and ________ there would be some ________ that need to be sorted out further ________.

Carter: I understand but USD 3000 should get you a half ________. You know paying USD 3000 for the car and USD 5000 to get the ________ replaced is just ________. If I knew this early, I would not ________ this car. You can take the car. I just want my ________ back.

卡特：我懂，可是三千塊應該可以買到還可以的車。你說花了三千元買車再花五千元換引擎是不是很蠢。早知道是這樣我才不會碰這台車。你把車拿回去，我只要把錢拿回來就好。

UNIT 14

車窗被砸

▶▶影子跟讀「短對話」練習 MP3 014

此篇為**「影子跟讀短對話練習」**，此章節規劃了由聽**「短對話」**的shadowing練習，能從最基礎、最易上手的部分切入新多益聽力備考並提升考生的專注力，現在就一起動身，開始聽**「短對話」**！

Jennifer: I knew that was you. I saw you walking up and down the street after I parked the car.

珍妮佛：我知道是你幹的！我停好車之後有看到你在街上閒逛。

Roy: It wasn't me! I didn't do it. How dare you accuse me for something like that, I do have a problem with you but I am not that nasty.

羅伊：真的不是我，我沒有做！你怎麼可以誣賴我會做這樣的事。我是跟你有過節可是我沒有這麼惡劣。

Jennifer: Why were you being sneaky then?

珍妮佛：那你為什麼鬼鬼祟祟的？

Roy: What sneaky! I was just taking a walk, what's that got to do with you?

羅伊：我哪有鬼鬼祟祟！我只是在散步，這干你什麼事？

Jennifer: Cut the crap! I don't believe anything comes out of your mouth. You think I got no proof, let me call the police and pull out the footage of the surveillance camera. Let's see what else you got to say. Just let me tell you, if you were caught doing it, you'd better watch your ass.

珍妮佛：少來！我才不相信你講的話。你以為我沒有證據，等我叫警察來調出監視器的畫面，到時候看你有什麼好說。我跟你說，如果真的抓到是你做，你就給我小心一點！

UNIT ⓮

車窗被砸

▶▶「短對話」填空練習 MP3 014

除了前面的**「影子跟讀短對話練習」**，現在試著在聽完對話後，完成下列對話中填空部分，從中強化生活場景中常見的字彙以及拼字能力，答案的話請參照前面的對話喔！

Jennifer: I knew that was you. I saw you walking up and down ________ after I parked ________.	**珍妮佛**：我知道是你幹的！我停好車之後有看到你在街上閒逛。
Roy: It wasn't me! I didn't do it. How dare you ________ me for something like that, I do have a problem with you but I am not that ________.	**羅伊**：真的不是我，我沒有做！你怎麼可以誣賴我會做這樣的事。我是跟你有過節可是我沒有這麼惡劣。
Jennifer: Why were you being ________ then?	**珍妮佛**：那你為什麼鬼鬼祟祟的？

Roy: What sneaky! I was just taking a walk, what's that got to do with you?

羅伊：我哪有鬼鬼祟祟！我只是在散步，這干你什麼事？

Jennifer: __________! I don't believe anything comes out of __________. You think I got no __________, let me call the __________ and pull out the __________ of the __________ camera. Let's see what else you got to say. Just let me tell you, if you were caught doing it, you'd better __________ your ass.

珍妮佛：少來！我才不相信你講的話。你以為我沒有證據，等我叫警察來調出監視器的畫面，到時候看你有什麼好說。我跟你說，如果真的抓到是你做，你就給我小心一點！

UNIT ⑮

預約看醫生

▶▶影子跟讀「短對話」練習 MP3 015

此篇為**「影子跟讀短對話練習」**，此章節規劃了由聽**「短對話」**的shadowing練習，能從最基礎、最易上手的部分切入新多益聽力備考並提升考生的專注力，現在就一起動身，開始聽**「短對話」**！

Tony: Hello, I am calling to check whether there is a vacancy for Dr. Howard to see me this morning. I am not feeling 100 %.

湯尼：您好，我想問一下能不能掛哈沃醫生今天早上的門診？我覺得非常不舒服。

Nurse Chelsea: Hang on a second, I will check his availability. Well, I am sorry he is fully booked today.

護士雀兒喜：請等一下，我查一下預約紀錄。嗯，不好意思他今天都約滿了。

Tony: What about other doctors? Maybe Dr. Abbott?

湯尼：那其他醫生呢？查一下亞伯特醫生好嗎？

Nurse Chelsea: He is also fully booked unfortunately.

護士雀兒喜：很可惜他也約滿了。

Tony: Can I ask for a huge favour please? I know you don't normally do this, but would you please take my contact details and call me back if any of the vacancies come up? I would be home all day. Any time is a good time as long as I get to see a doctor today. I live very close, I can be there within 10 mins.

湯尼：我可以請您幫個大忙嗎？我知道你們通常不會這樣做，可是您是不是可以留下我的聯絡方式，如果有人取消請通知我好嗎？我整天都會在家，所以什麼時間都可以，只要看的到醫生就好。我住得很近，十分鐘就能到。

UNIT ⑮

預約看醫生

▶▶「短對話」填空練習 MP3 015

除了前面的**「影子跟讀短對話練習」**，現在試著在聽完對話後，完成下列對話中填空部分，從中強化生活場景中常見的字彙以及拼字能力，答案的話請參照前面的對話喔！

Tony: Hello, I am calling to ________ whether there is a ________ for Dr.Howard to see me this ________. I am not feeling 100 %.	**湯尼：**您好，我想問一下能不能掛哈沃醫生今天早上的門診？我覺得非常不舒服。
Nurse Chelsea: Hang on ________, I will check his ________. Well, I am sorry he is ________ today.	**護士雀兒喜：**請等一下，我查一下預約紀錄。嗯，不好意思他今天都約滿了。
Tony: What about other________? Maybe Dr. Abbott?	**湯尼：**那其他醫生呢？查一下亞伯特醫生好嗎？

Nurse Chelsea: He is also ________ unfortunately.

護士雀兒喜：很可惜他也約滿了。

Tony: Can I ask for a ________ favour please? I know you don't ________ do this, but would you please take my ________ and call me back if any of the ________ come up? I would be ________ all day. Any time is a good time as long as I get to see ________ today. I live very close. I can be there within 10 mins.

湯尼：我可以請您幫個大忙嗎？我知道你們通常不會這樣做，可是您是不是可以留下我的聯絡方式，如果有人取消請通知我好嗎？我整天都會在家，所以什麼時間都可以，只要看的到醫生就好。我住得很近，十分鐘就能到。

UNIT 16

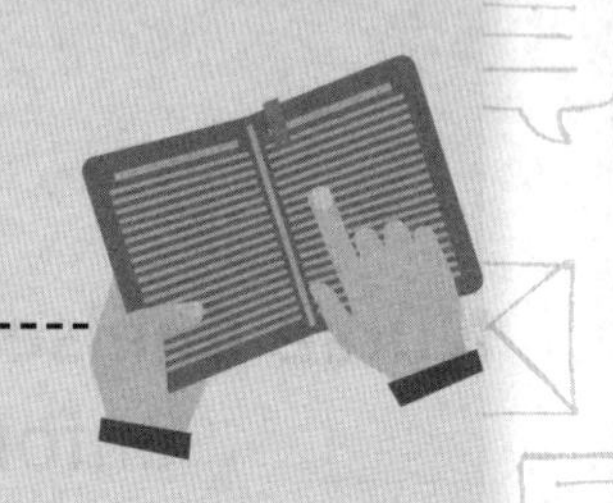

有人插隊

▶▶影子跟讀「短對話」練習 MP3 016

此篇為**「影子跟讀短對話練習」**，此章節規劃了由聽**「短對話」**的shadowing練習，能從最基礎、最易上手的部分切入新多益聽力備考並提升考生的專注力，現在就一起動身，開始聽**「短對話」**！

Campbell: Hey, are you done yet? Just pick one and move out of the way, I am trying to get through here.

坎伯：嘿！你有完沒完，隨便選一個然後趕快讓開，我要過去。

Carrie: Excuse me, mind your language! I am sorry my trolley got in your way, I will move it for you, but you don't have to be so rude. I am just doing my shopping here.

凱莉：什麼！你講話好聽一點好嘛！很抱歉我推車擋到你的路，我會讓路給你可是你也不用這麼沒禮貌，我也只不過是來買東西。

Campbell: I am sorry if I came across as rude. I am just not myself today. Things are not exactly going my way today, so now I've made it worse. My apologies.

坎伯：對不起如果你覺得我是個很無理的人，我今天不知道是怎麼回事，做什麼事都不順利，現在更糟了。請接受我的道歉。

Carrie: Apology accepted. I feel for you, but it is not my fault. Now I am having a bad day because I got yelled at by a complete stranger.

凱莉：沒關係。我很同情你，可是你不順並不是我的錯，我無端端被一個不認識的人罵，那不是換我倒楣嗎？

UNIT 16

有人插隊

「短對話」填空練習 MP3 016

除了前面的**「影子跟讀短對話練習」**，現在試著在聽完對話後，完成下列對話中填空部分，從中強化生活場景中常見的字彙以及拼字能力，答案的話請參照前面的對話喔！

Campbell: Hey, are you done yet? Just pick one and move out of ________, I am trying to get through here.	**坎伯：**嘿！你有完沒完，隨便選一個然後趕快讓開，我要過去。
Carrie: Excuse me, mind your ________! I am sorry my ________ got in your way, I will move it for you, but you don't have to be ________. I am just doing my ________ here.	**凱莉：**什麼！你講話好聽一點好嘛！很抱歉我推車擋到你的路，我會讓路給你可是你也不用這麼沒禮貌，我也只不過是來買東西。

Campbell: I am sorry if I ____ ______ as rude. I am just not myself today. Things are not ________ going my way today, so now I've made it worse. My apologies.

坎伯：對不起如果你覺得我是個很無理的人，我今天不知道是怎麼回事，做什麼事都不順利，現在更糟了。請接受我的道歉。

Carrie: Apology accepted. I feel for you, but it is not my fault. Now I am having a bad day because I got yelled at by a ________.

凱莉：沒關係。我很同情你，可是你不順並不是我的錯，我無端端被一個不認識的人罵，那不是換我倒楣嗎？

UNIT 17

申請表填錯

▶▶影子跟讀「短對話」練習 MP3 017

此篇為**「影子跟讀短對話練習」**，此章節規劃了由聽**「短對話」**的shadowing練習，能從最基礎、最易上手的部分切入新多益聽力備考並提升考生的專注力，現在就一起動身，開始聽**「短對話」**！

Christine: I am sorry I just realized I made a mistake on the application. I meant to take General training, but I accidently picked Academic. Is it possible for me to change now?	**克莉絲汀：**不好意思我剛才發現我的申請表填錯了，我應該要選一般訓練組，可是我誤選了學術組。請問可以更換嗎？
Mark: Well, you should have been more careful while you are filling it out.	**馬克：**嗯，你填表的時候應該小心一點。
Christine: I am really sorry,	**克莉絲汀：**我真的很抱歉，

but I really do need to take General training, because there is no hope in hell I would pass Academic.

可是我真的需要考一般訓練組，因為我絕對不可能通過學術組的考試。

Mark: I would suggest you check in as is and if we have any cancellations from General training, we can swap you over. Often we do have a few noshows, but there is no guarantee.

馬克：我會建議你先以學術組的身分入場，如果有一般訓練組的考生沒來，我們再把你換過去。通常都會有人缺考，但這無法保證。

Christine: Well, thanks for the advice. I think I would go ahead and get checked in for now, but please keep it in mind that I need to swap. That will be much appreciated.

克莉絲丁：嗯，謝謝你的建議，我就照這樣先入場，再麻煩你記得我需要更換。真的很感謝你。

UNIT 17

申請表填錯

「短對話」填空練習 MP3 017

除了前面的**「影子跟讀短對話練習」**，現在試著在聽完對話後，完成下列對話中填空部分，從中強化生活場景中常見的字彙以及拼字能力，答案的話請參照前面的對話喔！

Christine: I am sorry I just realized I made __________ on the __________. I meant to take General __________, but I accidently picked __________. Is it possible for me to __________ now?

克莉絲汀：不好意思我剛才發現我的申請表填錯了，我應該要選一般訓練組，可是我誤選了學術組。請問可以更換嗎？

Mark: Well, you should have been more __________ while you are __________ it out.

馬克：嗯，你填表的時候應該小心一點。

Christine: I am really sorry,

克莉絲汀：我真的很抱歉，

but I really do ________ to take General training, because there is no ________ in hell I would pass ________.

可是我真的需要考一般訓練組，因為我絕對不可能通過學術組的考試。

Mark: I would suggest you ________ as is and if we have any ________ from General training, we can ________ you over. Often we do have a few noshows, but there is no ________.

馬克：我會建議你先以學術組的身分入場，如果有一般訓練組的考生沒來，我們再把你換過去。通常都會有人缺考，但這無法保證。

Christine: Well, thanks for the ________. I think I would ________ and get checked in for now, but please keep it in mind that I need to swap. That will be much ________.

克莉絲丁：嗯，謝謝你的建議，我就照這樣先入場，再麻煩你記得我需要更換。真的很感謝你。

UNIT 18

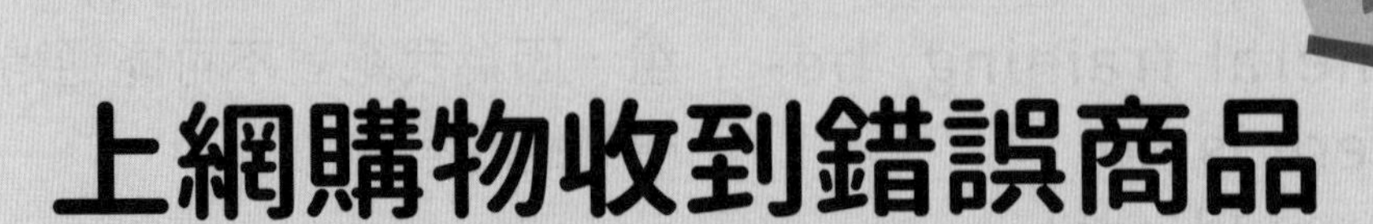

上網購物收到錯誤商品

▶▶影子跟讀「短對話」練習 MP3 018

此篇為**「影子跟讀短對話練習」**，此章節規劃了由聽**「短對話」**的shadowing練習，能從最基礎、最易上手的部分切入新多益聽力備考並提升考生的專注力，現在就一起動身，開始聽**「短對話」**！

Alison: Hi, I ordered a pair of shoes, but what I received is the wrong size.

艾利森：您好，我有訂購一雙鞋，可是我收到的尺寸是錯的。

Timothy: Sure I can organise an exchange for you. What size are you after?

提摩西：好的，我立刻幫您換貨，請問您要哪一個尺寸？

Alison: Oh perhaps I didn't make myself clear. What I was trying to say is, there is a mix up, I ordered a size 24 and on the documentation it also stated size 24, but I actually received size 22 in-

艾利森：我可能沒有說清楚，我是想說，我訂的是24號，文件上也是24號，可是實際上我收到的是22號。我的訂單號碼是：332448。

stead. My order number is #332448.

Timothy: Right, sorry for the inconvenience caused. If you can organize the item and the paperwork to be sent back to us, we will organize the exchange for you.

提摩西：好的，對您造成的不便很抱歉，如果你可以連鞋子還有文件一起寄回來的話，我們會幫您換貨。

Alison: Do I have to pay for the postage?

艾利森：那我要付郵資嗎？

Timothy: Yes, that's correct, but you will not be charged again the postage for us to send the right one for you.

提摩西：是的，可是你不需要付我們寄回去的郵資。

Alison: I don't think it is fair, because it was negligence on your side. Why am I liable for the return postage? That's a scam.

艾利森：這不公平吧！因為這是你們的疏忽為什麼我要付寄回去的郵資？這是搶人吧！

UNIT ⑱

上網購物收到錯誤商品

▶▶「短對話」填空練習 MP3 018

除了前面的**「影子跟讀短對話練習」**，現在試著在聽完對話後，完成下列對話中填空部分，從中強化生活場景中常見的字彙以及拼字能力，答案的話請參照前面的對話喔！

Alison: Hi, I ordered a pair of __________, but what I received is the __________.

艾利森：您好，我有訂購一雙鞋，可是我收到的尺寸是錯的。

Timothy: Sure I can organise __________ for you. What size are you after?

提摩西：好的，我立刻幫您換貨，請問您要哪一個尺寸？

Alison: Oh perhaps I didn't make myself clear. What I was trying to say is, there is a __________, I ordered a __________ and on the __________ it also stated size 24, but I actually received size 22 in-

艾利森：我可能沒有說清楚，我是想說，我訂的是24號，文件上也是24號，可是實際上我收到的是22號。我的訂單號碼是：332448。

stead. My order ________ is #332448.

Timothy: Right, sorry for the ________ caused. If you can ________ the item and the ________ to be sent back to us, we will organize the ________ for you.

提摩西：好的，對您造成的不便很抱歉，如果你可以連鞋子還有文件一起寄回來的話，我們會幫您換貨。

Alison: Do I have to pay for the ________?

艾利森：那我要付郵資嗎？

Timothy: Yes, that's ________, but you will not be charged again the postage for us to ________ the right one for you.

提摩西：是的，可是你不需要付我們寄回去的郵資。

Alison: I don't think it is fair, because it was ________ on your side. Why am I liable for the ________? That's a ________.

艾利森：這不公平吧！因為這是你們的疏忽為什麼我要付寄回去的郵資？這是搶人吧！

UNIT 19

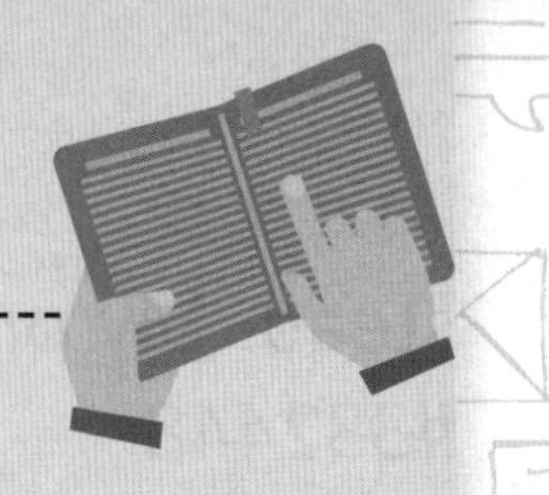

找工作

▶▶ 影子跟讀「短對話」練習 MP3 019

此篇為**「影子跟讀短對話練習」**，此章節規劃了由聽**「短對話」**的shadowing練習，能從最基礎、最易上手的部分切入新多益聽力備考並提升考生的專注力，現在就一起動身，開始聽**「短對話」**！

Jennifer: Yes, we are looking for seasonal workers for cucumber picking, have you done any farm work before?

珍妮佛：是的，我們有在徵採小黃瓜的臨時工，你有做過農場的工作嗎？

Arthur: I am afraid not, but I am very hardworking. I was wondering how much do you pay and whether the room and board are included?

亞瑟：不好意思沒有，可是我很認真，我想請問時薪是多少？有包吃住嗎？

Jennifer: Well, it is $22 an hour before tax. There is a

珍妮佛：嗯，扣稅之前是每個小時 22 塊，農場上有一

shed on the farm where you can stay for free, but you have to supply your own food. How soon can you start?

個農舍你要的話可以免費住，可是食物要自己買。你什麼時候可以開始上班？

Arthur: I can start anytime but the problem is, I don't have a clue how to get there, I am in Brisbane right now, and I rely on public transportation.

亞瑟：我隨時都可以開始，可是有一個問題，我不知道要怎麼去那裡，我目前在布里斯本，我只能搭大眾交通工具。

Jennifer: My suggestion is to hop on a greyhound bus to Bundaberg. Give me a call before you arrive. I can pick you up from the terminal.

珍妮佛：我建議你搭灰狗巴士到邦達堡，你到之前先打電話給我，我到車站去接你。

UNIT ⓳

找工作

▶▶「短對話」填空練習 MP3 019

除了前面的**「影子跟讀短對話練習」**，現在試著在聽完對話後，完成下列對話中填空部分，從中強化生活場景中常見的字彙以及拼字能力，答案的話請參照前面的對話喔！

Jennifer: Yes, we are looking for ____________ workers for ___________ picking, have you done any ____________ work before?	**珍妮佛：**是的，我們有在徵採小黃瓜的臨時工，你有做過農場的工作嗎？
Arthur: I am afraid not, but I am very ____________. I was wondering how much do you pay and whether the ____________ and board are included?	**亞瑟：**不好意思沒有，可是我很認真，我想請問時薪是多少？有包吃住嗎？
Jennifer: Well, it is $22 _______	**珍妮佛：**嗯，扣稅之前是每

____ before tax. There is a shed on the farm where you can stay for free, but you have to supply your own food. How soon can you start?

個小時 22 塊，農場上有一個農舍你要的話可以免費住，可是食物要自己買。你什麼時候可以開始上班？

Arthur: I can start anytime but the problem is, I don't have ________ how to get there, I am in ________ right now, and I rely on ________.

亞瑟：我隨時都可以開始，可是有一個問題，我不知道要怎麼去那裡，我目前在布里斯本，我只能搭大眾交通工具。

Jennifer: My ________ is to hop on a ________ bus to Bundaberg. Give me a call before you arrive. I can pick you up from the ________.

珍妮佛：我建議你搭灰狗巴士到邦達堡，你到之前先打電話給我，我到車站去接你。

UNIT 20

住宿

▶▶影子跟讀「短對話」練習 MP3 020

此篇為**「影子跟讀短對話練習」**，此章節規劃了由聽**「短對話」**的shadowing練習，能從最基礎、最易上手的部分切入新多益聽力備考並提升考生的專注力，現在就一起動身，開始聽**「短對話」**！

Mark: I understand you do not welcome a smoker, but I think having a good tenant is far more important.

馬克：我知道你不歡迎抽菸的人，可是我覺得找到一個好的房客才是最重要的。

Ann: I know what you are trying to say, but I really don't want to ruin the new carpet. We only just had it put in last year.

安：我懂你的意思，可是我真的不想把我的新地毯給毀了，我們去年才換過。

Mark: Well, what about if I keep the smoke away from

馬克：嗯，那如果我不在房間抽菸呢？我只在房子外面

the room, I will only smoke when I am outside of the house. Would you consider to take me in under that condition?

抽，這樣的話你會考慮讓我搬進來嗎？

Ann: I personally would be happy with it, but I need to speak to my husband before I can confirm with you.

安：我個人來説是可以接受，可是我還是要問一下我先生，才能跟你確認。

Mark: I promise you can count on me. Plus I am only here for a short time, I would try to stay out of your way.

馬克：我保證我會守信用。何況我只是租短期，我盡量不讓你添麻煩。

UNIT 20

住宿

▶▶「短對話」填空練習 MP3 020

除了前面的**「影子跟讀短對話練習」**，現在試著在聽完對話後，完成下列對話中填空部分，從中強化生活場景中常見的字彙以及拼字能力，答案的話請參照前面的對話喔！

Mark: I _________ you do not welcome a _________, but I think having a good tenant is far more _________.	**馬克：**我知道你不歡迎抽菸的人，可是我覺得找到一個好的房客才是最重要的。
Ann: I know what you are trying to say, but I really don't want to _________ the new _________. We only just had it put in last year.	**安：**我懂你的意思，可是我真的不想把我的新地毯給毀了，我們去年才換過。
Mark: Well, what about if I keep the smoke away from	**馬克：**嗯，那如果我不在房間抽菸呢？我只在房子外面

the room, I will only smoke when I am ________ of the house. Would you consider to take me in under that ____ ______?

抽，這樣的話你會考慮讓我搬進來嗎？

Ann: I ________ would be happy with it, but I need to speak to my ________ before I can ________ you.

安：我個人來說是可以接受，可是我還是要問一下我先生，才能跟你確認。

Mark: I promise you can ____ ______ me. Plus I am only here for a short time, I would try to ________ of your way.

馬克：我保證我會守信用。何況我只是租短期，我盡量不讓你添麻煩。

UNIT 21

沒拿到薪水

▶▶影子跟讀「短對話」練習 MP3 021

此篇為**「影子跟讀短對話練習」**，此章節規劃了由聽**「短對話」**的shadowing練習，能從最基礎、最易上手的部分切入新多益聽力備考並提升考生的專注力，現在就一起動身，開始聽**「短對話」**！

Erin: Hey Felice, just a quick word. I was under the assumption the pay day is every Thursday, but I still haven't received my pay for the past two weeks.

艾倫：嗨，菲莉絲，我可以跟你談一下嗎？我們不是每個星期四發薪水嗎？可是我到現在都還沒收到前兩個禮拜的薪水。

Felice: Is that right? The pay period is actually every two weeks, but you should have received it by now. I am pretty sure I have signed it off to the payroll last week. Let me check with them for you.

菲莉絲：是嗎？我們都是兩個星期才發一次，可是你也應該收到了才對。我記得我上星期已經簽出去給薪資部了，我幫你查一下。

Erin: Thanks for that. I really need the money to pay the bills.	**艾倫**：謝謝你，我真的急著用錢。
Felice: I just spoke to payroll, apparently your bank detail is incorrect, and the payment has been bounced back. If you can head over there to fix that up today, the payment should be in your account by next Thursday.	**菲莉絲**：我剛跟薪資部門確認過，你的銀行帳號不正確，所以錢被退回來了。如果你今天過去那裡修改的話，應該下星期四就會進你的帳戶了。

UNIT 21

沒拿到薪水

▶▶「短對話」填空練習 MP3 021

除了前面的**「影子跟讀短對話練習」**，現在試著在聽完對話後，完成下列對話中填空部分，從中強化生活場景中常見的字彙以及拼字能力，答案的話請參照前面的對話喔！

Erin: Hey Felice, just a ______ ____ word. I was under the __ ________ the pay day is every __________, but I still haven't ___________ my pay for the past __________ weeks.	**艾倫：**嗨，菲莉絲，我可以跟你談一下嗎？我們不是每個星期四發薪水嗎？可是我到現在都還沒收到前兩個禮拜的薪水。
Felice: Is that right? The ____ ______ is actually every two weeks, but you should have received it __________. I am pretty sure I have signed it off to __________ last week. Let me check with them for	**菲莉絲：**是嗎？我們都是兩個星期才發一次，可是你也應該收到了才對。我記得我上星期已經簽出去給薪資部了，我幫你查一下。

you.

Erin: Thanks for that. I really need the __________ to pay the bills.

艾倫：謝謝你，我真的急著用錢。

Felice: I just spoke to payroll, apparently your bank detail is __________, and the payment has been __________ back. If you can head over there to __________ that up today, the payment should be in your __________ by next __________.

菲莉絲：我剛跟薪資部門確認過，你的銀行帳號不正確，所以錢被退回來了。如果你今天過去那裡修改的話，應該下星期四就會進你的帳戶了。

UNIT 22

被騙

▶▶影子跟讀「短對話」練習 MP3 022

此篇為**「影子跟讀短對話練習」**，此章節規劃了由聽**「短對話」**的shadowing練習，能從最基礎、最易上手的部分切入新多益聽力備考並提升考生的專注力，現在就一起動身，開始聽**「短對話」**！

Freddy: Hey Jennifer, can I quickly check my last time sheet, please? The payment doesn't seem to add up.	**佛瑞迪：**嘿，珍妮佛，我可以看一下我上一次的班表嗎？薪水怪怪的。
Jennifer: What's wrong with it?	**珍妮佛：**是怎麼樣怪？
Freddy: I kept a record for the hours I worked since I started, I should get 1800 dollars this pay, but I only got 1750 dollars. I don't get it.	**佛瑞迪：**我從第一天就有紀錄上班的時數，我這次的薪水應該是 1 8 0 0元，可是怎麼只有 1750元，我真的不懂。

Jennifer: The 50 dollars were deducted for the utility bill.

珍妮佛：50 塊是拿來扣水電費的。

Freddy: You told me I can stay for free. You should have made it clear before I started. I feel like a fool.

佛瑞迪：你說我可以免費住的，我開工前你應該講清楚，我真的覺得被耍了！

Jennifer: Well, there's no such thing as a free lunch. Take it or leave it.

珍妮佛：嗯，你應該知道天下沒有白吃的午餐，要不要隨便你。

Freddy: I have no problem paying for what I used, but I do have problems with you not being upfront with me.

佛瑞迪：要我付水電費是沒問題，可是我的問題是你不坦白跟我說。

UNIT 22

被騙

▶▶「短對話」填空練習 MP3 022

除了前面的**「影子跟讀短對話練習」**，現在試著在聽完對話後，完成下列對話中填空部分，從中強化生活場景中常見的字彙以及拼字能力，答案的話請參照前面的對話喔！

Freddy: Hey Jennifer, can I quickly check my last ______ ____, please? The payment doesn't seem to _________.

佛瑞迪：嘿，珍妮佛，我可以看一下我上一次的班表嗎？薪水怪怪的。

Jennifer: What's wrong with it?

珍妮佛：是怎麼樣怪？

Freddy: I kept a record for the hours I worked since I started, I should get 1800 dollars this pay, but I only got 1750 dollars. I don't _______

佛瑞迪：我從第一天就有紀錄上班的時數，我這次的薪水應該是 1 8 0 0元，可是怎麼只有 1750元，我真的不懂。

__.

Jennifer: The 50 dollars were ________ for the ________.	**珍妮佛：**50 塊是拿來扣水電費的。
Freddy: You told me I can stay ________. You should have made it clear before I started. I feel like ________.	**佛瑞迪：**你說我可以免費住的，我開工前你應該講清楚，我真的覺得被耍了！
Jennifer: Well, there's no such thing as ________. Take it or leave it.	**珍妮佛：**嗯，你應該知道天下沒有白吃的午餐，要不要隨便你。
Freddy: I have no ________ paying for what I used, but I do have problems with you not being ________ with me.	**佛瑞迪：**要我付水電費是沒問題，可是我的問題是你不坦白跟我說。

UNIT 23

換工作

▶▶ 影子跟讀「短對話」練習 MP3 023

此篇為**「影子跟讀短對話練習」**，此章節規劃了由聽**「短對話」**的shadowing練習，能從最基礎、最易上手的部分切入新多益聽力備考並提升考生的專注力，現在就一起動身，開始聽**「短對話」**！

Teddy: I don't know a better way to bring this up. Well, I've got a job lined up in Melbourne and I need to jump on the next available flight. So tomorrow will be my last day.

泰迪：我不知道該怎樣開口，嗯，我在墨爾本找到工作，我需要馬上離開，所以明天是我的最後一天。

Jennifer: You can't do this to me, I need people here, too. You told me that you need to give me at least two weeks notice if you are leaving.

珍妮佛：你怎麼可以這樣，我這裡也需要人，我跟你說過如果你要走，至少要給我兩個星期的通知。

Teddy: What can I do? They want me to start next week!	**泰迪：**我能怎麼辦，他們叫我下星期就開工！
Jennifer: That would have to wait then. I really don't appreciate people screwing me over.	**珍妮佛：**那也只能等了，我最不喜歡別人來這套。
Teddy: What if I just leave tomorrow?	**泰迪：**那我如果明天就走怎麼辦？
Jennifer: You won't see a cent of your pay.	**珍妮佛：**那你就別想拿到薪水。
Teddy: Well, if that's the case, I will stay for two weeks. Please take this as my resignation.	**泰迪：**好吧，如果是這樣的話，我也只能等兩個星期了，那這樣就算你有收到我的離職通知了吧！

UNIT 23

換工作

▶▶「短對話」填空練習 MP3 023

除了前面的**「影子跟讀短對話練習」**，現在試著在聽完對話後，完成下列對話中填空部分，從中強化生活場景中常見的字彙以及拼字能力，答案的話請參照前面的對話喔！

Teddy: I don't know a better way to ________ this up. Well, I've got a job lined up in Melbourne and I need to jump on the next available flight. So tomorrow will be my last day.

泰迪：我不知道該怎樣開口，嗯，我在墨爾本找到工作，我需要馬上離開，所以明天是我的最後一天。

Jennifer: You can't do this to me, I need ________ here, too. You told me that you need to give me at least ____ ______ notice if you are leaving.

珍妮佛：你怎麼可以這樣，我這裡也需要人，我跟你說過如果你要走，至少要給我兩個星期的通知。

Teddy: What can I do? They want me to start ________!

泰迪：我能怎麼辦，他們叫我下星期就開工！

Jennifer: That would have to wait then. I really don't ____ ______ people screwing me over.

珍妮佛：那也只能等了，我最不喜歡別人來這套。

Teddy: What if I just leave __ ________?

泰迪：那我如果明天就走怎麼辦？

Jennifer: You won't see ____ ______ of your pay.

珍妮佛：那你就別想拿到薪水。

Teddy: Well, if that's the case, I will stay for two weeks. Please take this as my ________.

泰迪：好吧，如果是這樣的話，我也只能等兩個星期了，那這樣就算你有收到我的離職通知了吧！

UNIT 24

車禍

▶▶影子跟讀「短對話」練習 MP3 024

此篇為**「影子跟讀短對話練習」**，此章節規劃了由聽**「短對話」**的shadowing練習，能從最基礎、最易上手的部分切入新多益聽力備考並提升考生的專注力，現在就一起動身，開始聽**「短對話」**！

Paul: What do you think you are doing? You can't just cut in like this without indicating! Look you made a dent on the panel. Luckily, no one was injured, but you freaked me out!	**保羅：**你在幹嘛！你不能沒有打燈就切進來！你看板金都凹進去了，還好沒有人受傷，可是我嚇到了！
Kirsten: I didn't see you there. You were at my blind spot!	**柯絲汀：**我沒有看到你，你在我的盲點。
Paul: There is no excuse. You	**保羅：喔，**這不是藉口，你

should be more careful when you are driving! Focus on the road! I am in a rush and the car is still drivable, I think I will just grab your contact details and let the insurance company deal with it.

開車的時候本來就要小心！注意路況！我現在趕著要走，車也還能開，不然我就先拿你的聯絡資料再請保險公司處理。

Kirsten: There is a problem, I am only a traveler here and this car is not insured. I don't know what to do. I think we need to call the police.

柯絲汀：這有點問題，我只是觀光客，車還沒有保險。我真不知道該怎麼辦，我看還是叫警察吧！

Paul: Well, you are in deep trouble then. You will have to pay for it with your own moncy. This will teach you a lesson.

保羅：嗯，你糟了你，你要用你自己的錢付，這會讓你學到教訓的。

Kirsten: it might not be my fault. Let's get the police in-volved.

柯絲汀：這不一定是我的錯，讓警察處理吧！

UNIT 24

車禍

▶▶「短對話」填空練習 MP3 024

除了前面的**「影子跟讀短對話練習」**，現在試著在聽完對話後，完成下列對話中填空部分，從中強化生活場景中常見的字彙以及拼字能力，答案的話請參照前面的對話喔！

Paul: What do you ________ you are doing? You can't just cut in like this without indicating! Look you made ______ ____ on the ________. Luckily, no one was ________, but you freaked me out!	**保羅：**你在幹嘛！你不能沒有打燈就切進來！你看板金都凹進去了，還好沒有人受傷，可是我嚇到了！
Kirsten: I didn't see you there. You were at my ________!	**柯絲汀：**我沒有看到你，你在我的盲點。
Paul: There is no excuse. You should be more ________	**保羅：**喔，這不是藉口，你開車的時候本來就要小心！

when you are driving! Focus on the ________! I am in a rush and the car is still ________, I think I will just grab your contact details and let the ________ company deal with it.

注意路況！我現在趕著要走，車也還能開，不然我就先拿你的聯絡資料再請保險公司處理。

Kirsten: There is a problem, I am only a ________ here and this car is not insured. I don't know what to do. I think we need to call ________.

柯絲汀：這有點問題，我只是觀光客，車還沒有保險。我真不知道該怎麼辦，我看還是叫警察吧！

Paul: Well, you are in ________ then. You will have to pay for it with your own money. This will teach you ________.

保羅：嗯，你糟了你，你要用你自己的錢付，這會讓你學到教訓的。

Kirsten: it might not be my fault. Let's get the police involved.

柯絲汀：這不一定是我的錯，讓警察處理吧！

UNIT 25

租車

▶▶影子跟讀「短對話」練習 MP3 025

此篇為**「影子跟讀短對話練習」**，此章節規劃了由聽**「短對話」**的shadowing練習，能從最基礎、最易上手的部分切入新多益聽力備考並提升考生的專注力，現在就一起動身，開始聽**「短對話」**！

Oscar: Hi, this is Oscar and I meant to bring back the Ford Focus by close of business today, but we are caught in traffic at the moment, there is no way I will make it there in time.

奧斯卡：嗨！你好，我本來今天下班之前要把福特的Focus 還回去，可是我們現在卡在車陣中，我不可能及時趕到。

Jennifer: Thanks for letting us know, in that case you will be charged for an extra day.

珍妮佛：謝謝你跟我們説，那樣的話你必須多付一天的錢。

Oscar: I know, that's what I

奧斯卡：我知道，這也是我

am calling for. I will only be a few hours late. Is there some kind of late fee that I can pay instead of paying for the entire day?

打電話給你的理由，我只是遲幾個小時而已，有沒有可能我們付遲到的費用就好？不要收我們一天的錢？

Jennifer: Unfortunately, there will be no one here after 5pm.

珍妮佛：不好意思，我們5點下班之後就沒有人在辦公室了。

Oscar: Is it possible to return the car at your other office at the airport since it's open 24/7?

奧斯卡：那我們能不能把車改到你機場的辦公室還，因為是開 24 小時的？

Jennifer: That can be arranged, but you still will be paying for the late fee and the location charge.

珍妮佛：這我們可以安排，可是你還是要付遲到的費用，還有乙地還車的費用。

UNIT 25

租車

▶▶「短對話」填空練習 MP3 025

除了前面的**「影子跟讀短對話練習」**，現在試著在聽完對話後，完成下列對話中填空部分，從中強化生活場景中常見的字彙以及拼字能力，答案的話請參照前面的對話喔！

Oscar: Hi, this is Oscar and I meant to bring back the ____ ______ by close of ________ today, but we are caught in __________ at the moment, there is no way I will make it there _________.	**奧斯卡：**嗨！你好，我本來今天下班之前要把福特的 Focus 還回去，可是我們現在卡在車陣中，我不可能及時趕到。
Jennifer: Thanks for letting us know, in that case you will be __________ for an extra day.	**珍妮佛：**謝謝你跟我們說，那樣的話你必須多付一天的錢。

Oscar: I know, that's what I am ________. I will only be a few hours late. Is there some kind of ________ that I can pay instead of paying for the ________?

奧斯卡：我知道，這也是我打電話給你的理由，我只是遲幾個小時而已，有沒有可能我們付遲到的費用就好？不要收我們一天的錢？

Jennifer: ________, there will be no one here after 5pm.

珍妮佛：不好意思，我們5點下班之後就沒有人在辦公室了。

Oscar: Is it possible to ________ the car at your other office at the ________ since it's open 24/7?

奧斯卡：那我們能不能把車改到你機場的辦公室還，因為是開24小時的？

Jennifer: That can be ________, but you still will be paying for the late fee and the ________.

珍妮佛：這我們可以安排，可是你還是要付遲到的費用，還有乙地還車的費用。

UNIT 26

分擔油錢

▶▶ 影子跟讀「短對話」練習 MP3 026

此篇為**「影子跟讀短對話練習」**，此章節規劃了由聽**「短對話」**的shadowing練習，能從最基礎、最易上手的部分切入新多益聽力備考並提升考生的專注力，現在就一起動身，開始聽**「短對話」**！

Scott: Hi, I saw your message that you are looking for someone to chip in the petrol to go to Perth. I was wondering when are you going exactly?

史考特：你好，我有看到你的貼文說要找人分擔油錢一起開車到伯斯？我想請問你什麼時候要去？

Jennifer: I am aiming to get there before middle of next month, but I am pretty flexible if the timing doesn't suit you.

珍妮佛：我計畫下個月中前要到，可是我蠻彈性的，如果時間不適合你的話，我們可以再談。

Scott: How long are you planning to be on the road? I still got work to do for the next week and a half. I can leave on the 10th if that's ok with you.

史考特：你打算要開幾天？我目前還要在工作一個半星期。如果你同意的話，我可以 10 號出發。

Jennifer: I would prefer to depart earlier, but I guess I can wait for you. I am in no hurry.

珍妮佛：我是希望早一點出發可是沒關係，我可以等你，反正我也不急。

Scott: So the petrol will be 50-50?

史考特：那油錢是一人一半?

Jennifer: Well, that's one thing I want to point out, I think it would be fair if you could cover 60 and I cover 40 since the car is mine. Would this work for you?

魯賓：嗯，我想跟你先說清楚，我覺得既然車也是我出得化的話，我出四成你出六成比較公平，這樣你可以接受嗎？

UNIT 26

分擔油錢

「短對話」填空練習 MP3 026

除了前面的**「影子跟讀短對話練習」**，現在試著在聽完對話後，完成下列對話中填空部分，從中強化生活場景中常見的字彙以及拼字能力，答案的話請參照前面的對話喔！

Scott: Hi, I saw your __________ that you are looking for __________ to chip in the petrol to go to __________. I was wondering when are you going exactly?

史考特：你好，我有看到你的貼文說要找人分擔油錢一起開車到伯斯？我想請問你什麼時候要去？

Jennifer: I am aiming to get there before __________ of next __________, but I am pretty __________ if the timing doesn't suit you.

珍妮佛：我計畫下個月中前要到，可是我蠻彈性的，如果時間不適合你的話，我們可以再談。

Scott: How long are you planning to be on ________? I still got work to do for the next week and a half. I can __ ________ on the 10th if that's ok with you.

史考特：你打算要開幾天？我目前還要在工作一個半星期。如果你同意的話，我可以 10 號出發。

Jennifer: I would prefer to __ ________ earlier, but I guess I can wait for you. I am in ____ ______.

珍妮佛：我是希望早一點出發可是沒關係，我可以等你，反正我也不急。

Scott: So the ________ will be 50-50?

史考特：那油錢是一人一半?

Jennifer: Well, that's one thing I want to point out, I think it would be ________ if you could cover 60 and I cover 40 since ________ is mine. Would this work for you?

魯賓：嗯，我想跟你先說清楚，我覺得既然車也是我出得化的話，我出四成你出六成比較公平，這樣你可以接受嗎？

UNIT 27

開車被臨檢

▶▶ 影子跟讀「短對話」練習 MP3 027

此篇為**「影子跟讀短對話練習」**，此章節規劃了由聽**「短對話」**的shadowing練習，能從最基礎、最易上手的部分切入新多益聽力備考並提升考生的專注力，現在就一起動身，開始聽**「短對話」**！

Jim: I have been signaling for you to stop, why didn't you stop?	**吉姆**：我一直指示你要停下來，你為什麼還一直開？
Carla: Sorry, I wasn't sure you are after me.	**卡拉**：抱歉我不知道你是在追我。
Jim: You almost caused an accident back there, why were you doing 50 at a 70 zone? Are you under the influence?	**吉姆**：你知道你剛差點造成車禍嗎？為什麼你在限速 70 的路段開 50? 你是嗑藥還是喝酒？

Carla: No, of course not! I thought I was being careful by driving slowly.	**卡拉：**不，當然沒有！我只是覺得開慢一點會比較安全。
Jim: You were holding up traffic, and people were trying to overtake you, that is rather dangerous. Can I have your license please?	**吉姆：**你造成交通堵塞，大家都不斷地超車，這很危險。請給我看你的駕照？
Carla: Here you go. This is my international license and passport.	**卡拉：**拿去，這是我的國際駕照還有護照。
Jim: I suppose the road rules are similar in your country. You've got to keep up with the traffic and don't slow down all of a sudden. Just be more aware from now on.	**吉姆：**我想交通規則在每個國家應該都差不多，你一定要跟上車流，不要突然慢下來，麻煩你從現在開始要多注意。

UNIT 27

開車被臨檢

▶▶「短對話」填空練習 MP3 027

除了前面的「**影子跟讀短對話練習**」，現在試著在聽完對話後，完成下列對話中填空部分，從中強化生活場景中常見的字彙以及拼字能力，答案的話請參照前面的對話喔！

Jim: I have been ________ for you to stop, why didn't you stop?	**吉姆**：我一直指示你要停下來，你為什麼還一直開？
Carla: Sorry, I wasn't sure you are after me.	**卡拉**：抱歉我不知道你是在追我。
Jim: You almost caused an __ ________ back there, why were you doing 50 at a 70 zone? Are you under the ____ ______?	**吉姆**：你知道你剛差點造成車禍嗎？為什麼你在限速 70 的路段開 50? 你是嗑藥還是喝酒？

Carla: No, of course not! I thought I was being _________ by driving slowly.

卡拉：不，當然沒有！我只是覺得開慢一點會比較安全。

Jim: You were holding up _________, and people were trying to overtake you, that is rather _________. Can I have your _________ please?

吉姆：你造成交通堵塞，大家都不斷地超車，這很危險。請給我看你的駕照？

Carla: Here you go. This is my _________ license and _________.

卡拉：拿去，這是我的國際駕照還有護照。

Jim: I suppose the road _________ are _________ in your country. You've got to keep up with the _________ and don't slow down all of a sudden. Just be more aware from now on.

吉姆：我想交通規則在每個國家應該都差不多，你一定要跟上車流，不要突然慢下來，麻煩你從現在開始要多注意。

UNIT 28

看醫生沒有保險

▶▶ 影子跟讀「短對話」練習 MP3 028

此篇為**「影子跟讀短對話練習」**，此章節規劃了由聽**「短對話」**的shadowing練習，能從最基礎、最易上手的部分切入新多益聽力備考並提升考生的專注力，現在就一起動身，開始聽**「短對話」**！

Miranda: Hello, I am feeling sick and I would like to see a doctor.

米蘭達：你好，我不太舒服，我想看醫生。

Gayle: Have you been here before?

蓋兒：你以前來過嗎？

Miranda: No, I am a tourist and I don't have travel insurance, can you tell me roughly how much it would cost?

米蘭達：沒有，我是觀光客，我沒有旅遊保險，你可以跟我說這樣大概要多少錢嗎？

Gayle: Seeing a doctor would be expensive without insurance.

蓋兒：看醫生沒有保險是很貴的。

Miranda: I developed a fever last night, and my body is aching, I just don't know what to do.

米蘭達：我昨天晚上開始發燒，我全身痠痛，我不知道要怎麼辦？

Gayle: I would suggest if it is not a life threatening condition, you can try to go to the drugstore and get to the over the counter medication. I mean, you are heading back in a few days, aren't you?

蓋兒：我會建議你，如果不是攸關性命的症狀，你可以先去藥局買成藥。我是說，你應該沒幾天就會回國了吧？不是嗎？

Miranda: Thanks, I will give it a try. I think it is just a cold, and it will go away in a few days.

米蘭達：謝謝，我去試試看，我想應該是感冒，希望它幾天就會好了。

UNIT 28

看醫生沒有保險

▶▶「短對話」填空練習 MP3 028

除了前面的**「影子跟讀短對話練習」**，現在試著在聽完對話後，完成下列對話中填空部分，從中強化生活場景中常見的字彙以及拼字能力，答案的話請參照前面的對話喔！

Miranda: Hello, I am feeling sick and I would like to see ________.	**米蘭達**：你好，我不太舒服，我想看醫生。
Gayle: Have you been here before?	**蓋兒**：你以前來過嗎？
Miranda: No, I am ________ and I don't have ________, can you tell me roughly how much it would cost?	**米蘭達**：沒有，我是觀光客，我沒有旅遊保險，你可以跟我說這樣大概要多少錢嗎？

Gayle: Seeing a doctor would be __________ without insurance.

蓋兒：看醫生沒有保險是很貴的。

Miranda: I developed __________ last night, and my body is aching, I just don't know what to do.

米蘭達：我昨天晚上開始發燒，我全身痠痛，我不知道要怎麼辦？

Gayle: I would suggest if it is not a life threatening __________, you can try to go to the __________ and get to the over the counter __________. I mean, you are __________ in a few days, aren't you?

蓋兒：我會建議你，如果不是攸關性命的症狀，你可以先去藥局買成藥。我是說，你應該沒幾天就會回國了吧？不是嗎？

Miranda: Thanks, I will give it a try. I think it is just a cold, and it will go away in a few days.

米蘭達：謝謝，我去試試看，我想應該是感冒，希望它幾天就會好了。

UNIT 29

沒趕上飛機

▶▶影子跟讀「短對話」練習 MP3 029

此篇為**「影子跟讀短對話練習」**，此章節規劃了由聽**「短對話」**的shadowing練習，能從最基礎、最易上手的部分切入新多益聽力備考並提升考生的專注力，現在就一起動身，開始聽**「短對話」**！

Colin: Hi, I was meant to be on the 12:30 flight to Miami. I am running really late, can you please check in for me?	**柯林**：您好，我應該是要搭 12:30 的飛機到邁阿密，我已經遲到了，您可不可以讓我先登記？
Janet: Come with me to the counter.	**珍娜**：請跟我到這個櫃台。
Colin: Thanks, you are my saviour!	**柯林**：太感謝了，你真是我的救星！
Janet: Don't speak too soon.	**珍娜**：話別說得太早，登機

The gate is about to close in 10 mins, and the check-in for that flight was just closed. I have to check with my supervisor to see if we are allowed to check you in.

門在十分鐘就要關了，基本上這班飛機的登記櫃台已經關了，我需要跟我的經理談一下是不是能夠讓你搭這班飛機。

Colin: Please help me out, I really have to make this flight because I've got a cruise booked in Miami departing tomorrow morning. I know that I am to be blamed for it. I should have been here earlier. But let's just look at the situation now.

柯林：求求你幫幫我，我真的必須搭上那班飛機，因為我明天早上還要從邁阿密出發搭郵輪。我知道遲到是我的錯，我真的應該早點來，可是先不要追究，重點是專注在現在的情況。

Janet: I can't say you are safe now. I will do my best to help you.

珍娜：我不敢保證一定可以幫你，可是我會盡力。

UNIT 29

沒趕上飛機

▶▶「短對話」填空練習 MP3 029

除了前面的**「影子跟讀短對話練習」**，現在試著在聽完對話後，完成下列對話中填空部分，從中強化生活場景中常見的字彙以及拼字能力，答案的話請參照前面的對話喔！

Colin: Hi, I was meant to be on the 12:30 flight to ______ ____. I am running really late, can you please check in for me?

柯林：您好，我應該是要搭 12:30 的飛機到邁阿密，我已經遲到了，您可不可以讓我先登記？

Janet: Come with me to the _________.

珍娜：請跟我到這個櫃台。

Colin: Thanks, you are my __ _______!

柯林：太感謝了，你真是我的救星！

Janet: Don't speak too soon. The gate is about to close in 10 mins, and the check-in for that ________ was just closed. I have to check with my ________ to see if we are allowed to check you in.

珍娜：話別說得太早，登機門在十分鐘就要關了，基本上這班飛機的登記櫃台已經關了，我需要跟我的經理談一下是不是能夠讓你搭這班飛機。

Colin: Please help me out, I really have to make this flight because I've got a ________ booked in Miami departing ________ morning. I know that I am to be ________ for it. I should have been here earlier. But let's just look at the ________ now.

柯林：求求你幫幫我，我真的必須搭上那班飛機，因為我明天早上還要從邁阿密出發搭郵輪。我知道遲到是我的錯，我真的應該早點來，可是先不要追究，重點是專注在現在的情況。

Janet: I can't say you are ________ now. I will do my best to help you.

珍娜：我不敢保證一定可以幫你，可是我會盡力。

UNIT 30

飯店換房間

▶▶ 影子跟讀「短對話」練習 MP3 030

此篇為**「影子跟讀短對話練習」**，此章節規劃了由聽**「短對話」**的shadowing練習，能從最基礎、最易上手的部分切入新多益聽力備考並提升考生的專注力，現在就一起動身，開始聽**「短對話」**！

Anita: Hi, I am the guest in Room 305. I made a complaint not long ago to complain the guest next door has been very noisy, but they still keep going, nothing has been done.

安妮塔： 您好， 我是305房的客人，我剛剛打過電話來抱怨隔壁的房客實在太吵了，可是他們到現在還在狂歡，沒有人去解決。

Sean: We are truly sorry. We did send someone over to speak to the guests. They promised that they will keep the volume down. We will send someone over again

西恩：我們真的很抱歉，我們的確有派人過去跟房客勸說了，他們有答應要小聲一點，我們馬上再派人過去。

shortly.

Anita: I don't know how effective that would be. It is late and I am exhausted, all I want to do is get some sleep. Why don't you look up whether there is another room that you can move me to. I am happy to change the room.

安妮塔：我不覺得會有什麼用，現在已經很晚了，我也很累了，我只想休息。你可以看看你們有沒有其他房間可以讓我換過去嗎？我情願換房間。

Sean: Sure thing, you can have Room 505. Anything else I can help you with?

西恩：沒問題，你可以換到 505 號房。還有其他事我們可以幫你服務的嗎？

UNIT 30

飯店換房間

▶▶「短對話」填空練習 MP3 030

除了前面的**「影子跟讀短對話練習」**，現在試著在聽完對話後，完成下列對話中填空部分，從中強化生活場景中常見的字彙以及拼字能力，答案的話請參照前面的對話喔！

Anita: Hi, I am the ________ in Room 305. I made a ________ not long ago to ________ the guest next door has been very noisy, but they still keep going, nothing has been done.

安妮塔：您好，我是305 房的客人，我剛剛打過電話來抱怨隔壁的房客實在太吵了，可是他們到現在還在狂歡，沒有人去解決。

Sean: We are truly sorry. We did send someone over to speak to the guests. They ________ that they will keep the ________ down. We will send someone over again __

西恩：我們真的很抱歉，我們的確有派人過去跟房客勸説了，他們有答應要小聲一點，我們馬上再派人過去。

________.

Anita: I don't know how ____ ______ that would be. It is late and I am ________, all I want to do is get some sleep. Why don't you ________ whether there is another __ ________ that you can move me to. I am happy to change the room.

安妮塔：我不覺得會有什麼用，現在已經很晚了，我也很累了，我只想休息。你可以看看你們有沒有其他房間可以讓我換過去嗎？我情願換房間。

Sean: ________, you can have Room 505. Anything else I can help you with?

西恩：沒問題，你可以換到 505 號房。還有其他事我們可以幫你服務的嗎？

UNIT 31

取消訂房

▶▶ 影子跟讀「短對話」練習 MP3 031

此篇為**「影子跟讀短對話練習」**，此章節規劃了由聽**「短對話」**的shadowing練習，能從最基礎、最易上手的部分切入新多益聽力備考並提升考生的專注力，現在就一起動身，開始聽**「短對話」**！

Lucas: Hello, I've got a room reserved for today under the name of Lucas Chow, but I am stuck in the Grand Canyon at the moment. I won't get in until tomorrow. My room has been pre-paid, but I was wondering whether I could push the booking by a day late.

路卡斯：您好，我今天有訂房，是以路卡斯州的名義。可是我現在卡在大峽谷，我要明天才會到。我的房間已經付清了，可是我想問問看我是不是可以把日期延後一天在入住？

Jodi: Let me check the details of your booking. Well, unfortunately you booked the ear-

僑蒂：讓我看一下你的訂房資料，嗯，不好意思你訂的是早鳥專案，是不能退款或

ly bird deal which is non-refundable and non-transferrable. I am afraid that if you don't check in today, you will still be charged.

轉讓的。如果你今天沒有入住的話，恐怕就浪費了。

Lucas: But I was caught out by the bad weather. The highway is shut down and there is nothing I can do.

路卡斯：可是我是被壞天氣困住，公路都封路了，這不是我能控制的。

Jodi: I am really sorry to hear that, I will suggest you bring this up to your insurance company. Some of travel insurance policy would cover it.

僑蒂：真的很抱歉，我只能建議你跟你的保險公司談談，有些旅行保險是有包含這種損失的。

UNIT 31

取消訂房

「短對話」填空練習 MP3 031

除了前面的**「影子跟讀短對話練習」**，現在試著在聽完對話後，完成下列對話中填空部分，從中強化生活場景中常見的字彙以及拼字能力，答案的話請參照前面的對話喔！

Lucas: Hello, I've got __________ reserved for today under the name of Lucas Chow, but I am __________ in the Grand Canyon at the moment. I won't get in until __________. My room has been pre-paid, but I was wondering whether I could push the booking by a day late.	**路卡斯：**您好，我今天有訂房，是以路卡斯州的名義。可是我現在卡在大峽谷，我要明天才會到。我的房間已經付清了，可是我想問問看我是不是可以把日期延後一天在入住？
Jodi: Let me check the details of your __________. Well, unfortunately you booked the	**僑蒂：**讓我看一下你的訂房資料，嗯，不好意思你訂的是早鳥專案，是不能退款或

early bird deal which is ______ ______ and __________. I am afraid that if you don't check in today, you will still be ______ ______.

轉讓的。如果你今天沒有入住的話，恐怕就浪費了。

Lucas: But I was caught out by the __________. The ______ ____ is shut down and there is nothing I can do.

路卡斯：可是我是被壞天氣困住，公路都封路了，這不是我能控制的。

Jodi: I am really sorry to hear that, I will __________ you bring this up to your insurance company. Some of ______ ______ policy would cover it.

僑蒂：真的很抱歉，我只能建議你跟你的保險公司談談，有些旅行保險是有包含這種損失的。

UNIT 32

不滿意旅行團的服務

▶▶ 影子跟讀「短對話」練習 MP3 032

此篇為**「影子跟讀短對話練習」**，此章節規劃了由聽**「短對話」**的shadowing練習，能從最基礎、最易上手的部分切入新多益聽力備考並提升考生的專注力，現在就一起動身，開始聽**「短對話」**！

Heather: I like the tourist attractions we visited, but in general I think there is definitely room for improvement.	**海瑟**：我喜歡我們去的那些景點，可是整體來說是還有很大的改善空間。
Maurice: How so?	**毛利斯**：怎麼說呢？
Heather: You've got to admit it, the hotel that we stayed in last night was so dated, and the mattress was so uncomfortable.	**海瑟**：你必須要承認，昨天晚上我們待的那個飯店好舊，而且床墊好不舒服。

Maurice: I know the hotel can do with a makeover, but it is still functional.

毛利斯：我知道那間飯店外觀需要整修一下，可是還是可以使用。

Heather: Don't get me started on the food. It is so basic, even our so called deluxe seafood BBQ last night. There were only a handful of the shrimps and some squid rings which is barely enough to go around. There is nothing fancy about this tour, you should rename it a budget tour. I know I signed up for a midrange comfort tour, but this is definitely more a budget one.

海瑟：更不要說餐點了，全部都好基本，就連昨天晚上所謂的海鮮總匯燒烤也只不過有幾隻蝦跟魷魚圈，根本都不夠吃。整趟旅程下來沒什麼特別的，應該更名為廉價旅行團。我知道，我參加的是中等的舒適團，可是這感覺上就像廉價團。

UNIT 32

不滿意旅行團的服務

▶▶ 「短對話」填空練習　MP3 032

除了前面的**「影子跟讀短對話練習」**，現在試著在聽完對話後，完成下列對話中填空部分，從中強化生活場景中常見的字彙以及拼字能力，答案的話請參照前面的對話喔！

Heather: I like the ________ attractions we visited, but in general I think there is ______ ____ room for improvement.	**海瑟**：我喜歡我們去的那些景點，可是整體來說是還有很大的改善空間。
Maurice: How so?	**毛利斯**：怎麼說呢？
Heather: You've got to ______ ____ it, the __________ that we stayed in last night was so dated, and the ___________ was so ________.	**海瑟**：你必須要承認，昨天晚上我們待的那個飯店好舊，而且床墊好不舒服。

Maurice: I know the hotel can do with a __________, but it is still __________.

毛利斯：我知道那間飯店外觀需要整修一下，可是還是可以使用。

Heather: Don't get me started on the food. It is so basic, even our so called deluxe __________ BBQ last night. There were only a handful of the __________ and some __________ which is barely enough to go around. There is nothing fancy about this __________, you should __________ it a __________ tour. I know I signed up for a __________ comfort tour, but this is definitely more a budget one.

海瑟：更不要說餐點了，全部都好基本，就連昨天晚上所謂的海鮮總匯燒烤也只不過有幾隻蝦跟魷魚圈，根本都不夠吃。整趟旅程下來沒什麼特別的，應該更名為廉價旅行團。我知道，我參加的是中等的舒適團，可是這感覺上就像廉價團。

UNIT 33

迷路

▶▶影子跟讀「短對話」練習 MP3 033

此篇為**「影子跟讀短對話練習」**，此章節規劃了由聽**「短對話」**的shadowing練習，能從最基礎、最易上手的部分切入新多益聽力備考並提升考生的專注力，現在就一起動身，開始聽**「短對話」**！

Mary: Hello, I am having trouble to find the Metropolitan museum, would you be able to point out the general direction for me, please?	**瑪莉：**你好，我一直找不到大都會博物館，你可以跟我説大概的方向在哪裡嗎？
Eason: Metropolitan museum!? You are a long way away from it. I guess you got off the subway too early. It will take you at least half an hour to get there on foot.	**伊森：**大都會博物館？！還很遠唉！我猜你應該是太早下地鐵了，如果走過去也至少要半個小時。

Mary: Right, what would you suggest I do?

瑪莉：那你會建議我怎麼做？

Eason: I think the easiest way would be to cut through Central Park until you run into 5th Ave then turn right. You should have no trouble finding it once you are on 5th Ave.

伊森：我覺得最容易的方式就是切過中央公園，一直到第五大道，在第五大道右轉。如果你到了第五大道，你就一定找的到。

Mary: Thanks for your help, I have been running around in circles for the past twenty minutes trying to find my way. I should have asked someone sooner.

瑪莉：謝謝你的幫忙，我已經原地打轉二十分鐘了還找不到。我應該早點問人的。

UNIT 33

迷路

▶▶「短對話」填空練習 MP3 033

除了前面的**「影子跟讀短對話練習」**，現在試著在聽完對話後，完成下列對話中填空部分，從中強化生活場景中常見的字彙以及拼字能力，答案的話請參照前面的對話喔！

Mary: Hello, I am having trouble to find the Metropolitan ________, would you be able to point out the general direction for me, please?	**瑪莉：**你好，我一直找不到大都會博物館，你可以跟我說大概的方向在哪裡嗎？
Eason: Metropolitan museum!? You are a long way away from it. I guess you got off the ________ too early. It will take you at least half ____ ______ to get there on foot.	**伊森：**大都會博物館？！還很遠唉！我猜你應該是太早下地鐵了，如果走過去也至少要半個小時。

Mary: Right, what would you suggest I do?

瑪莉：那你會建議我怎麼做？

Eason: I think the __________ way would be to cut through Central Park until you run into 5th Ave then turn right. You should have no __________ finding it once you are on 5th Ave.

伊森：我覺得最容易的方式就是切過中央公園，一直到第五大道，在第五大道右轉。如果你到了第五大道，你就一定找的到。

Mary: Thanks for your help, I have been running around in __________ for the past __________ minutes trying to find my way. I should have asked someone sooner.

瑪莉：謝謝你的幫忙，我已經原地打轉二十分鐘了還找不到。我應該早點問人的。

UNIT 34

錯過該搭的車

▶▶影子跟讀「短對話」練習 MP3 034

此篇為**「影子跟讀短對話練習」**，此章節規劃了由聽**「短對話」**的shadowing練習，能從最基礎、最易上手的部分切入新多益聽力備考並提升考生的專注力，現在就一起動身，開始聽**「短對話」**！

Mark: Look what happened! We just missed the bus!	**馬克**：你看看！我們真的錯過巴士了！
Sandy: That's ok, I am sure the next one will be here soon.	**珊蒂**：沒關係，我想下一班應該馬上就來了。
Mark: I think you really need to manage your time a bit better.	**馬克**：我覺得你應該善用你的時間。
Sandy: What do you mean?	**珊蒂**：你是什麼意思？

Mark: Well, if it wasn't for you taking your time curling your hair, we would have been on the bus as we speak.

馬克：嗯，如果不是因為你還在那邊慢慢捲頭髮，我們早就在巴士上了。

Sandy: Missing a bus is just a minor issue, but I really don't appreciate you criticising me like that. You can go to Universal Studio on your own, I much prefer to spend time with my hair curler.

珊蒂：沒搭上巴士只不過是件小事，但我真的很不喜歡你這樣批評我。你可以自己去環球影城，我情願回去慢慢捲我的頭髮。

Mark: I don't mean to offend you, but I only have a few days here in LA. I really want to make the most of it.

馬克：我不是故意要得罪你，可是我在洛杉磯只有幾天的時間，我真的想好好利用。

UNIT 34

錯過該搭的車

▶▶「短對話」填空練習 MP3 034

除了前面的**「影子跟讀短對話練習」**，現在試著在聽完對話後，完成下列對話中填空部分，從中強化生活場景中常見的字彙以及拼字能力，答案的話請參照前面的對話喔！

Mark: Look what happened! We just missed ________!	**馬克：**你看看！我們真的錯過巴士了！
Sandy: That's ok, I am sure the next one will be here soon.	**珊蒂：**沒關係，我想下一班應該馬上就來了。
Mark: I think you really need to ________ your time a bit better.	**馬克：**我覺得你應該善用你的時間。
Sandy: What do you mean?	**珊蒂：**你是什麼意思？

Mark: Well, if it wasn't for you taking your time __________ your hair, we would have been on __________ as we speak.

馬克：嗯，如果不是因為你還在那邊慢慢捲頭髮，我們早就在巴士上了。

Sandy: Missing a bus is just a __________ issue, but I really don't __________ you __________ me like that. You can go to __________ on your own, I much prefer to spend time with my __________ curler.

珊蒂：沒搭上巴士只不過是件小事，但我真的很不喜歡你這樣批評我。你可以自己去環球影城，我情願回去慢慢捲我的頭髮。

Mark: I don't mean to offend you, but I only have __________ days here in LA. I really want to make the most of it.

馬克：我不是故意要得罪你，可是我在洛杉磯只有幾天的時間，我真的想好好利用。

UNIT 35

折扣算錯

▶▶影子跟讀「短對話」練習 MP3 035

此篇為**「影子跟讀短對話練習」**，此章節規劃了由聽**「短對話」**的shadowing練習，能從最基礎、最易上手的部分切入新多益聽力備考並提升考生的專注力，現在就一起動身，開始聽**「短對話」**！

Troy: The total comes to 51.75 dollars.	**特洛伊：**總共是 51.75美金。
Melinda: Well, it doesn't seem right. My combo is 25 and the BBQ ribs on its own is 25. That should be 50 dollars, and we got a coupon for 10 percent off the total bill. I don't understand how did you get the total of 51.75?	**瑪琳達：**嗯，好像不太對，我的套餐是 25 元，單點碳烤肋排是 25 元。我有一張總價打九折的折價券，這樣怎麼會是51.75 元呢？
Troy: Yes, we did take 10	**特洛伊：**是的，我們已經把

percent off, but there is a 15 percent service charge applied to the total bill.	折扣算進去了，可是還要另外加一成五的服務費。
Melinda: Where did it say that?	**瑪琳達：**怎麼會，我沒有看到。
Troy: That's mentioned in the fine print.	**特洛伊：**明細裡有註明。
Melinda: Right, I didn't realize that. That's a lot!	**瑪琳達：**是嗎？我怎麼沒發現，這金額其實很大。
Troy: This must be your first time in the US. You will get your head around it pretty soon.	**特洛伊：**這你一定是第一次到美國。你很快就會知道的。
Melinda: I don't like the rule but what can I do!	**瑪琳達：**我並不喜歡這個規定，但我又能怎樣呢？

UNIT 35

折扣算錯

▶▶「短對話」填空練習 MP3 035

除了前面的**「影子跟讀短對話練習」**，現在試著在聽完對話後，完成下列對話中填空部分，從中強化生活場景中常見的字彙以及拼字能力，答案的話請參照前面的對話喔！

Troy: The ________ comes to ________ dollars.	**特洛伊：**總共是 51.75美金。
Melinda: Well, it doesn't seem right. My combo is 25 and the BBQ ribs on its own is 25. That should be ________, and we got a ________ for 10 percent off the ________. I don't understand how did you get the ________of 51.75?	**瑪琳達：**嗯，好像不太對，我的套餐是 25 元，單點碳烤肋排是 25 元。我有一張總價打九折的折價券，這樣怎麼會是51.75 元呢？

Troy: Yes, we did take 10 percent off, but there is a 15 percent ________ applied to the total bill.

特洛伊：是的，我們已經把折扣算進去了，可是還要另外加一成五的服務費。

Melinda: Where did it say that?

瑪琳達：怎麼會，我沒有看到。

Troy: That's mentioned in the fine print.

特洛伊：明細裡有註明。

Melinda: Right, I didn't realize that. That's a lot!

瑪琳達：是嗎？我怎麼沒發現，這金額其實很大。

Troy: This must be your first time in the US. You will get your head around it pretty soon.

特洛伊：這你一定是第一次到美國。你很快就會知道的。

Melinda: I don't like __________ but what can I do!

瑪琳達：我並不喜歡這個規定，但我又能怎樣呢？

UNIT 36

機場退稅

▶▶影子跟讀「短對話」練習 MP3 036

此篇為**「影子跟讀短對話練習」**，此章節規劃了由聽**「短對話」**的shadowing練習，能從最基礎、最易上手的部分切入新多益聽力備考並提升考生的專注力，現在就一起動身，開始聽**「短對話」**！

Marcie: Hi, here is the receipt for the refund.

瑪西：嗨！這是我要申請退稅的收據。

Joe: Thanks, can I look at the items please?

喬：謝謝，我可以看一下物品嗎？

Marcie: Oh no, I don't have them with me. I packed them all in my check-in.

瑪西：喔！糟糕！我沒有隨身帶著，我全部包在行李裡面。

Joe: We actually need to see the things you bought to ver-

喬：我們需要核對一下收據和商品。

ify against the receipt.

Marcie: Oh I am so sorry, I was not aware that I need to present them to you. I got my computer to carry and there is not much room left in my carry-on. Plus, one of the items is 100 ml of perfume, I am not allowed to have it as carry-on anyway. I swear to God I am a genuine tourist, I was just not aware of the rules. Please make an exception for me this time. I will remember it in the future.

瑪西：噢！我真的很抱歉，我不知道我需要拿商品給你看。我有一台電腦要帶，所以隨身行李沒什麼位子的。還有，我其中的一個商品是一瓶 100ml 的香水，我也沒辦法放進隨身行李裡。我發誓我真的只是單純的觀光客，我不清楚退稅的規定，是不是可以請您這次放我一馬，我以後一定會記得的。

UNIT 36

機場退稅

▶▶「短對話」填空練習 MP3 036

除了前面的**「影子跟讀短對話練習」**，現在試著在聽完對話後，完成下列對話中填空部分，從中強化生活場景中常見的字彙以及拼字能力，答案的話請參照前面的對話喔！

Marcie: Hi, here is the ______ ____ for the ________.	**瑪西**：嗨！這是我要申請退稅的收據。
Joe: Thanks, can I look at the ________ please?	**喬**：謝謝，我可以看一下物品嗎？
Marcie: Oh no, I don't have them with me. I ________ them all in my ________.	**瑪西**：喔！糟糕！我沒有隨身帶著，我全部包在行李裡面。
Joe: We actually need to see the things you bought to ____	**喬**：我們需要核對一下收據和商品。

______ against the __________.

Marcie: Oh I am so sorry, I was not aware that I need to __________ them to you. I got my __________ to carry and there is not much __________ left in my carry-on. Plus, one of the items is 100 ml of ____ ______, I am not allowed to have it as carry-on anyway. I swear to God I am a ________ __ tourist, I was just not aware of the rules. Please make an __________ for me this time. I will remember it in the future.

瑪西：噢！我真的很抱歉，我不知道我需要拿商品給你看。我有一台電腦要帶，所以隨身行李沒什麼位子的。還有，我其中的一個商品是一瓶 100ml 的香水，我也沒辦法放進隨身行李裡。我發誓我真的只是單純的觀光客，我不清楚退稅的規定，是不是可以請您這次放我一馬，我以後一定會記得的。

UNIT 37

上班遲到

▶▶影子跟讀「短對話」練習 MP3 037

此篇為**「影子跟讀短對話練習」**，此章節規劃了由聽**「短對話」**的shadowing練習，能從最基礎、最易上手的部分切入新多益聽力備考並提升考生的專注力，現在就一起動身，開始聽**「短對話」**！

Mary: Where the hell have you been? You are an hour late!	**瑪莉：**你跑到哪裡去了？遲到一個小時了。
Samuel: Hmmm....There was an accident on the highway, and the traffic was really backed up.	**山姆：**嗯，高速公路上出了車禍，所以很塞車。
Mary: Why didn't you call? You could have called and let us know. You know the orders have to go out by 7 am otherwise it won't get there in time. I had customers call-	**瑪莉：**為什麼你不打個電話來通知？你可以早點通知我們的！你知道訂單在七點前全部都要送出去，不然來不及。我正個早上都在接客戶抱怨的電話，我受夠了。

ing the whole morning to complain. I am really fed up with this.

Samuel: I am really sorry. I promise it won't happen again.

山姆：我很抱歉。我保證不再犯了。

Mary: This is getting ridiculous now. I can't put our reputation at risk.

瑪莉：這現在越來越可笑。我不能讓我們名聲蒙受風險。

Samuel: I know, I know. I haven't been reliable lately, but I promise I will be on time from now on. My orders will go out first thing in the morning.

山姆：我知道，我知道，我最近一直出狀況，我保證我現在開始一定會準時。訂單我一定優先處理。

Mary: Well, actions speak louder than words, prove it to me.

瑪莉：嗯！不要空口說白話，證明給我看。

UNIT 37

上班遲到

▶▶「短對話」填空練習 MP3 037

除了前面的**「影子跟讀短對話練習」**，現在試著在聽完對話後，完成下列對話中填空部分，從中強化生活場景中常見的字彙以及拼字能力，答案的話請參照前面的對話喔！

Mary: Where the hell have you been? You are ________ late!	**瑪莉：**你跑到哪裡去了？遲到一個小時了。
Samuel: Hmmm....There was an ________ on the ________, and the traffic was really backed up.	**山姆：**嗯，高速公路上出了車禍，所以很塞車。
Mary: Why didn't you call? You could have called and let us know. You know the ________ have to go out by 7 am otherwise it won't get there in time. I had ________ call-	**瑪莉：**為什麼你不打個電話來通知？你可以早點通知我們的！你知道訂單在七點前全部都要送出去，不然來不及。我正個早上都在接客戶抱怨的電話，我受夠了。

ing the whole morning to __ ________. I am really fed up with this.

Samuel: I am really sorry. I __ ________ it won't happen again.

山姆：我很抱歉。我保證不再犯了。

Mary: This is getting ________ __ now. I can't put our ______ ____ at risk.

瑪莉：這現在越來越可笑。我不能讓我們名聲蒙受風險。

Samuel: I know, I know. I haven't been __________ lately, but I promise I will be on time from now on. My orders will go out first thing in the morning.

山姆：我知道，我知道，我最近一直出狀況，我保證我現在開始一定會準時。訂單我一定優先處理。

Mary: Well, __________ speak louder than words, prove it to me.

瑪莉：嗯！不要空口說白話，證明給我看。

UNIT 38

忘記上司交代的事

▶▶影子跟讀「短對話」練習　MP3 038

此篇為**「影子跟讀短對話練習」**，此章節規劃了由聽**「短對話」**的shadowing練習，能從最基礎、最易上手的部分切入新多益聽力備考並提升考生的專注力，現在就一起動身，開始聽**「短對話」**！

Perry: I got my 2nd warning from Greg Johnson today, what a terrible way to start a day.	**派瑞**：我今天收到桂格強 森給的警告信，已經是第二份了。今天怎麼一早就這麼倒楣。
Mary: You've got to be kidding, what for?	**瑪莉**：開玩笑地吧！是為了什麼？
Perry: He asked me to look after the client last Friday, but I forgot to organize the pick-up for him. The client was upset and Greg is really	**派瑞**：他叫我負責上星期五的客戶拜訪，可是我忘了安排接機。客戶真的很不高興，所以桂格現在很氣我。

pissed off with me right now.

Mary: Oh, no. That's terrible. You know how much Greg values client relations. You are lucky you didn't get fired on the spot. You really need to get your act together.

瑪莉：喔，那真的很慘，你知道桂格很注重客戶關係的，你算很幸運，沒有當場被炒魷魚。你真的要用心一點。

Perry: It was a silly mistake. But I need to be on my best behaviour and lay low for a while. I can't afford to make any more mistakes, otherwise I will be gone in no time.

派瑞：這真的是很蠢的錯誤，我真的要發條上緊一點，暫時低調行事。不能再犯錯了，不然我應該很快就被炒了。

UNIT 38

忘記上司交代的事

▶▶「短對話」填空練習 MP3 038

除了前面的**「影子跟讀短對話練習」**，現在試著在聽完對話後，完成下列對話中填空部分，從中強化生活場景中常見的字彙以及拼字能力，答案的話請參照前面的對話喔！

Perry: I got my 2nd ________ __ from Greg Johnson today, what a ________ way to ___ ______ a day.	**派瑞：**我今天收到桂格強森給的警告信，已經是第二份了。今天怎麼一早就這麼倒楣。
Mary: You've got to be ______ ____, what for?	**瑪莉：**開玩笑地吧！是為了什麼？
Perry: He asked me to look after the _________ last ____ ______, but I forgot to ______ ____ the _________ for him. The client was _________ and	**派瑞：**他叫我負責上星期五的客戶拜訪，可是我忘了安排接機。客戶真的很不高興，所以桂格現在很氣我。

Greg is really pissed off with me _________.

Mary: Oh, no. That's terrible. You know how much Greg values _________. You are _________ you didn't get _________ on the spot. You really need to get your _________ together.

瑪莉：喔，那真的很慘，你知道桂格很注重客戶關係的，你算很幸運，沒有當場被炒鱿魚。你真的要用心一點。

Perry: It was a silly mistake. But I need to be on my best behaviour and lay low for a while. I can't afford to make any more mistakes, otherwise I will be gone in no time.

派瑞：這真的是很蠢的錯誤，我真的要發條上緊一點，暫時低調行事。不能再犯錯了，不然我應該很快就被炒了。

UNIT 39

護照弄丟重新申請

▶▶影子跟讀「短對話」練習 MP3 039

此篇為**「影子跟讀短對話練習」**，此章節規劃了由聽**「短對話」**的shadowing練習，能從最基礎、最易上手的部分切入新多益聽力備考並提升考生的專注力，現在就一起動身，開始聽**「短對話」**！

Jamie: Hello, I would like to file a police report about some stolen property.	**傑米：**您好，我想要報案，我的東西被偷了。
Mary: I can sort it out for you. Just need to get a few details off you. Can you talk me through about what hap-pened?	**瑪莉：**我可以幫你，只是需要你的一些資料，可以告訴我發生什麼事嗎？
Jamie: Someone cut my backpack open and stole my passport and camera, and I	**傑米：**有人把我的背包割開，偷了我的護照還有相機。我不確定是什麼時候發

am not exactly sure when it happened, but I can tell you the last time I saw my camera was about lunch time in Times Square.

生的，可是我可以跟你說我最後一次看到我的相機是大概中午的時候，在時代廣場。

Mary: Ok, I must tell you the chance is slim for the items to be found, but if you can fill out this form, then I will put it through to our system. The report number is TR00201653.

瑪莉：好的，我必須老實跟你說東西不太可能找的回來，可是如果你可以填完這張表格，我可以輸入在我們的系統內建檔，你的報案號碼是：TR00201653。

Jamie: Can I have a hard copy of the report, please? I need it for the embassy to issue a passport replacement for me.

傑米：可以印一張報案紀錄出來給我嗎？我需要紙本報告來申請新的護照。

UNIT 39

護照弄丟重新申請

▶▶「短對話」填空練習 MP3 039

除了前面的**「影子跟讀短對話練習」**，現在試著在聽完對話後，完成下列對話中填空部分，從中強化生活場景中常見的字彙以及拼字能力，答案的話請參照前面的對話喔！

Jamie: Hello, I would like to file a ________ about some stolen ________.

傑米：您好，我想要報案，我的東西被偷了。

Mary: I can ________ it out for you. Just need to get a few ________ off you. Can you talk me through about what happened?

瑪莉：我可以幫你，只是需要你的一些資料，可以告訴我發生什麼事嗎？

Jamie: Someone cut my ________ open and stole my ________ and ________, and I

傑米：有人把我的背包割開，偷了我的護照還有相機。我不確定是什麼時候發

am not ________ sure when it happened, but I can tell you the last time I saw my camera was about ________ time in Times ________.

生的，可是我可以跟你說我最後一次看到我的相機是大概中午的時候，在時代廣場。

Mary: Ok, I must tell you the ________ is ________ for the ________ to be found, but if you can ________ this ________, then I will put it through to our ________. The report number is ______ ________.

瑪莉：好的，我必須老實跟你說東西不太可能找的回來，可是如果你可以填完這張表格，我可以輸入在我們的系統內建檔，你的報案號碼是：TR00201653。

Jamie: Can I have a hard ____ ______ of the report, please? I need it for the ________ to issue a passport ________ for me.

傑米：可以印一張報案紀錄出來給我嗎？我需要紙本報告來申請新的護照。

UNIT 40

銷售能力

▶▶ 影子跟讀「短對話」練習 MP3 040

此篇為**「影子跟讀短對話練習」**，此章節規劃了由聽**「短對話」**的shadowing練習，能從最基礎、最易上手的部分切入新多益聽力備考並提升考生的專注力，現在就一起動身，開始聽**「短對話」**！

Mary: Do you know what bothers me the most?	**Mary**：你知道有一件事讓我不舒服嗎？
Jack: What is it?	**Jack**：什麼事？
Mary: As important as we are to the company, I can't believe there are sales reps that make more than us.	**Mary**：我們對公司這麼重要，竟然還有業務賺得比我們多。
Jack: Who makes more than us?	**Jack**： 誰賺得比我們多？

Mary: I think Luther makes more than us.

Mary：好像 Luther 賺得比我們多。

Jack: You know that Luther can sell ice to Eskimos right? His selling skill is insane! I'm fine with him making more than us if he's the only one.

Jack：你知道 Luther有能力賣冰塊給愛斯基摩人吧？他的銷售能力太強了！他賺得比我多我一點問題都沒有。

Mary: Yeah....but he is a sales rep!

Mary：是沒錯…可是他是個業務啊！

Jack: I am okay with it. We make the products and he sells them. The company wouldn't be profitable unless both of us are good at our jobs. So I think it is fair.

Jack：我覺得還好，我們做產品他們銷售。如果有一方做不好公司都不能賺錢，所以我覺得公平。

UNIT 40

銷售能力

「短對話」填空練習 MP3 040

除了前面的**「影子跟讀短對話練習」**，現在試著在聽完對話後，完成下列對話中填空部分，從中強化生活場景中常見的字彙以及拼字能力，答案的話請參照前面的對話喔！

Mary: Do you know what __ ________ me the most?	**Mary**：你知道有一件事讓我不舒服嗎？
Jack: What is it?	**Jack**：什麼事？
Mary: As __________ as we are to the __________, I can't believe there are __________ that make more than us.	**Mary**：我們對公司這麼重要，竟然還有業務賺得比我們多。
Jack: Who makes __________ us?	**Jack**：誰賺得比我們多？

Mary: I think Luther makes more than us.

Mary：好像 Luther 賺得比我們多。

Jack: You know that Luther can sell __________ to Eskimos right? His selling __________ is __________! I'm fine with him __________ more than us if he's the only one.

Jack：你知道 Luther有能力賣冰塊給愛斯基摩人吧？他的銷售能力太強了！他賺得比我多我一點問題都沒有。

Mary: Yeah....but he is a sales rep!

Mary：是沒錯…可是他是個業務啊！

Jack: I am okay with it. We make the __________ and he sells them. The company wouldn't be __________ unless both of us are __________ our jobs. So I think it is __________.

Jack：我覺得還好，我們做產品他們銷售。如果有一方做不好公司都不能賺錢，所以我覺得公平。

UNIT 41

動手不動口的人太多了

▶▶影子跟讀「短對話」練習 MP3 041

此篇為**「影子跟讀短對話練習」**，此章節規劃了由聽**「短對話」**的shadowing練習，能從最基礎、最易上手的部分切入新多益聽力備考並提升考生的專注力，現在就一起動身，開始聽**「短對話」**！

Mark: Just because I'm in charge of administration does not make me a servant. It seems like everyone can just walk into my office and tell me to do this or that. This company just has too many chiefs and not enough Indians！

Mark：就因為我是負責行政的不代表我是他們的僕人。好多時候這幫人隨意就走進我的辦公室，要我做這做那的，這家公司動嘴的人很多，但是做事的人太少了！

Tina: I'm so sorry, did you talk to your boss about it？

Tina：真是抱歉，你有跟老闆提起這件事嗎？

Mark: Yes I did and he said he will assign office assistants to every department, so I won't be the only one.

Mark：有，他說他會安排每一個部門有自己的行政同事，就不會一直找我了。

Tina: That sounds like a good plan！

Tina：這聽起來是個好方法！

UNIT 41

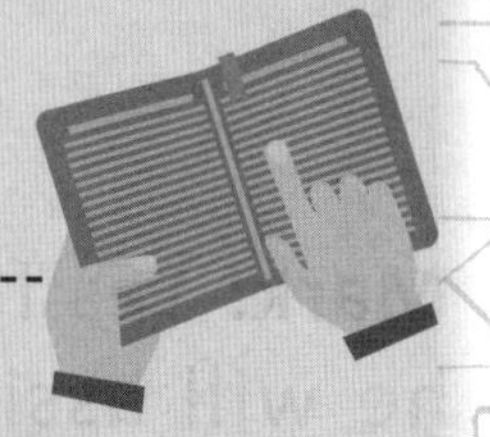

動手不動口的人太多了

▶▶「短對話」填空練習 MP3 041

除了前面的**「影子跟讀短對話練習」**，現在試著在聽完對話後，完成下列對話中填空部分，從中強化生活場景中常見的字彙以及拼字能力，答案的話請參照前面的對話喔！

Mark: Just because I'm in charge of ________ does not make me a ________. It seems like everyone can just walk into my ________ and tell me to do this or that. This ________ just has too many ________ and not enough ________!

Mark：就因為我是負責行政的不代表我是他們的僕人。好多時候這幫人隨意就走進我的辦公室，要我做這做那的，這家公司動嘴的人很多，但是做事的人太少了！

Tina: I'm so ________, did you talk to your ________ about it？

Tina：真是抱歉，你有跟老闆提起這件事嗎？

Mark: Yes I did and he said he will ________ office ____ ______ to every _________, so I won't be the only one.

Mark：有，他說他會安排每一個部門有自己的行政同事，就不會一直找我了。

Tina: That sounds like a ____ ______ plan！

Tina：這聽起來是個好方法！

UNIT 42

搞砸生意

▶▶影子跟讀「短對話」練習 MP3 042

此篇為**「影子跟讀短對話練習」**，此章節規劃了由聽**「短對話」**的shadowing練習，能從最基礎、最易上手的部分切入新多益聽力備考並提升考生的專注力，現在就一起動身，開始聽**「短對話」**！

Mary: Hey! Frank. Why the sad face?	**Mary**：嘿！Frank，臉色為什麼這麼糟？
Frank: I just blew a huge deal with this company, I was so close, but then they ran a final check on our product quality report and decided not to sign with us.	**Frank**：我剛剛搞砸了一個生意，我就差那麼一點點，但是最後他們再看了一次我們的產品質量報告後就決定不簽了。
Mary: Ouch! What is wrong with the report? Maybe it's not too late to salvage the	**Mary**：唉呀！那報告有什麼問題嗎？也許我們還有挽救的機會？

crisis?

Frank: I think it's hard because apparently the inspector described our facility more like a lab than manufacturing. That turned them off instantly.

Frank：我想有點難，那審核我們的人在報告上說我們的工廠比較像實驗室，不像生產廠房。這一點馬上就讓他們打退堂鼓了。

Mary: You could invite them to come take a look themselves and maybe they will change their minds.

Mary：你可以邀請他們自己來看一次啊！也許這會改變他們的想法。

Frank: Yeah, I suppose I can give it a shot. There really is no downside for asking.

Frank：我想也是，反正問一下也沒有壞處。

UNIT 42

搞砸生意

▶▶「短對話」填空練習 MP3 042

除了前面的**「影子跟讀短對話練習」**，現在試著在聽完對話後，完成下列對話中填空部分，從中強化生活場景中常見的字彙以及拼字能力，答案的話請參照前面的對話喔！

Mary: Hey! Frank. Why the __________?

Mary：嘿！Frank，臉色為什麼這麼糟？

Frank: I just blew a __________ with this __________, I was so __________, but then they ran a final __________ on our product __________ and decided not to __________ with us.

Frank：我剛剛搞砸了一個生意，我就差那麼一點點，但是最後他們再看了一次我們的產品質量報告後就決定不簽了。

Mary: Ouch! What is __________ with the report? Maybe

Mary：唉呀！那報告有什麼問題嗎？也許我們還有挽

it's not too late to __________ the __________?

救的機會？

Frank: I think it's hard because __________ the __________ described our __________ more like a __________ than __________. That turned them off instantly.

Frank：我想有點難，那審核我們的人在報告上說我們的工廠比較像實驗室，不像生產廠房。這一點馬上就讓他們打退堂鼓了。

Mary: You could __________ them to come take a look themselves and maybe they will __________ their __________.

Mary：你可以邀請他們自己來看一次啊！也許這會改變他們的想法。

Frank: Yeah, I __________ I can give it a __________. There really is no __________ for asking.

Frank：我想也是，反正問一下也沒有壞處。

UNIT 43

勝任團隊合作

▶▶影子跟讀「短對話」練習　MP3 043

此篇為**「影子跟讀短對話練習」**，此章節規劃了由聽**「短對話」**的shadowing練習，能從最基礎、最易上手的部分切入新多益聽力備考並提升考生的專注力，現在就一起動身，開始聽**「短對話」**！

Mary: How should I prepare for a job interview?

Mary：我要怎麼準備面試呢？

Brandon: Studying some of the common questions asked in an interview helps a lot.

Brandon：找一些很常出現的面試問題，這樣準備很有幫助。

Mary: How do I make sure that it's an answer they like?

Mary：我怎麼知道他們想要聽到什麼答案？

Brandon: There are a couple of things that all companies

Brandon：許多公司都喜歡聽到一些差不多的答案，比

like to hear during an interview. For example, all companies like to hear that you are a team player and you work well in a team setting. So if they ask you what your strengths are, besides mentioning what you are good at also try to include that you are a good team player.

如說所有的公司都喜歡聽你說你是一個以團隊為優先的人，而在任何團隊裡你都可以勝任。所以如果他們問你的強項是甚麼，除了講你專業上的東西，也可以順便提說你是一個以團隊為主的人。

Mary: Okay thanks!

Mary：了解了，謝謝！

UNIT 43

勝任團隊合作

▶▶「短對話」填空練習 MP3 043

除了前面的**「影子跟讀短對話練習」**，現在試著在聽完對話後，完成下列對話中填空部分，從中強化生活場景中常見的字彙以及拼字能力，答案的話請參照前面的對話喔！

Mary: How should I ________ __ for a ________?	**Mary**：我要怎麼準備面試呢？
Brandon: Studying some of the ________ questions asked in an ________ helps a lot.	**Brandon**：找一些很常出現的面試問題，這樣準備很有幫助。
Mary: How do I ________ sure that it's an ________ they like?	**Mary**：我怎麼知道他們想要聽到什麼答案？

Brandon: There are a __________ of things that all __________ like to hear during an interview. For example, all companies like to hear that you are a __________ and you work well in a __________ setting. So if they ask you what your __________ are, besides mentioning what you are __________ also try to __________ that you are a good team player.

Mary: Okay thanks!

Brandon：許多公司都喜歡聽到一些差不多的答案，比如說所有的公司都喜歡聽你說你是一個以團隊為優先的人，而在任何團隊裡你都可以勝任。所以如果他們問你的強項是甚麼，除了講你專業上的東西，也可以順便提說你是一個以團隊為主的人。

Mary：了解了，謝謝！

UNIT 44

做事抄捷徑

▶▶ 影子跟讀「短對話」練習 MP3 044

此篇為「**影子跟讀短對話練習**」，此章節規劃了由聽「**短對話**」的shadowing練習，能從最基礎、最易上手的部分切入新多益聽力備考並提升考生的專注力，現在就一起動身，開始聽「**短對話**」！

Mark: Cindy's way of doing things bothers me sometimes.	**Mark**：Cindy 做事的方法讓我有點感冒。
Laura: Really? I don't work with her enough to notice anything. What does she do that bothers you?	**Laura**：真的啊？我跟她不夠熟，她做了甚麼嗎？
Mark: It's the little things. She always cuts corners and tries to do things the fastest way but not necessarily the	**Mark**：都是一些小事情啦，她總是走捷徑想用最快，但不是最正確的方法來處理事情。她不知道雖然現

right way. She doesn't know that it might save her time now, but in the future we might not be able to find the proper data or file.

在省了點時間， 但是現在沒做好，以後可能會讓公司找不到檔案或數據。

Laura: I see. Did you talk to her about it? After all, she's just an intern. It is good for her if we tell her now to help her career.

Laura：我懂了，你有跟她溝通過嗎？她畢竟只是個實習生，現在跟她講對她的未來發展也比較好。

Mark: Good idea. I will do it this afternoon.

Mark：有道理，那我下午跟她講。

UNIT 44

做事抄捷徑

▶▶「短對話」填空練習 MP3 044

除了前面的**「影子跟讀短對話練習」**，現在試著在聽完對話後，完成下列對話中填空部分，從中強化生活場景中常見的字彙以及拼字能力，答案的話請參照前面的對話喔！

Mark: Cindy's way of doing things __________ me ___________.	**Mark**：Cindy 做事的方法讓我有點感冒。
Laura: Really? I don't work with her enough to __________ anything. What does she do that bothers you?	**Laura**：真的啊？我跟她不夠熟，她做了甚麼嗎？
Mark: It's the __________ things. She always __________ and tries to do things the fastest way but not __________	**Mark**：都是一些小事情啦，她總是走捷徑想用最快，但不是最正確的方法來處理事情。她不知道雖然現

__ the right way. She doesn't know that it might _________ her time now, but in the ____ _____ we might not be able to find the proper _________ or _________.

在省了點時間， 但是現在沒做好，以後可能會讓公司找不到檔案或數據。

Laura: I see. Did you talk to her about it? After all, she's just _________. It is good for her if we tell her now to help her _________.

Laura：我懂了，你有跟她溝通過嗎？她畢竟只是個實習生，現在跟她講對她的未來發展也比較好。

Mark: Good idea. I will do it this afternoon.

Mark：有道理，那我下午跟她講。

UNIT 45

生意談成的機會不高

▶▶ 影子跟讀「短對話」練習 MP3 045

此篇為**「影子跟讀短對話練習」**，此章節規劃了由聽**「短對話」**的shadowing練習，能從最基礎、最易上手的部分切入新多益聽力備考並提升考生的專注力，現在就一起動身，開始聽**「短對話」**！

Linda: What do you think about that company?	**Linda**：你覺得剛剛那家公司怎麼樣？
Sean: They are growing fast and just by looking at the office, their structure is solid and well-organized.	**Sean**：他們成長很快，剛剛看了一下他們辦公室感覺好像也很有制度。
Linda: I agree, they seem to have all the right elements of a good start-up company, but somehow I don't feel like	**Linda**：對啊，一家好的初創公司要有的元素好像他們都有，不過我覺得他們好像對我們的產品不太感興趣。

they like our products too much.	
Sean: I don't know about that. I think they try not to show too much interest to give us pressure on pricing.	**Sean**：我不知道。我認為他們是為了給我們談價上的壓力，才表現得沒那麼有興趣。
Linda: That is true, and they don't seem to be in a hurry to make the decision. Do you think we can get this business?	**Linda**：嗯，他們好像也沒有要那麼快做決定。你覺得我們這筆生意會談成嗎？
Sean: I think it's a long shot, but definitely possible.	**Sean**：有可能，但是現在看起來機率不高。

UNIT 45

生意談成的機會不高

▶▶「短對話」填空練習 MP3 045

除了前面的**「影子跟讀短對話練習」**，現在試著在聽完對話後，完成下列對話中填空部分，從中強化生活場景中常見的字彙以及拼字能力，答案的話請參照前面的對話喔！

Linda: What do you think about that __________?	**Linda**：你覺得剛剛那家公司怎麼樣？
Sean: They are growing _____ ______ and just by looking at the __________, their structure is solid and _________ __.	**Sean**：他們成長很快，剛剛看了一下他們辦公室感覺好像也很有制度。
Linda: I agree, they seem to have all the ___________ of a good ___________ company, but somehow I don't feel like	**Linda**：對啊，一家好的初創公司要有的元素好像他們都有，不過我覺得他們好像對我們的產品不太感興趣。

they like our __________ too much.

Sean: I don't know about that. I think they try not to show too much __________ to give us __________ on __________.

Sean：我不知道。我認為他們是為了給我們談價上的壓力，才表現得沒那麼有興趣。

Linda: That is __________, and they don't seem to be in a hurry to make the __________. Do you think we can get this __________?

Linda：嗯，他們好像也沒有要那麼快做決定。你覺得我們這筆生意會談成嗎？

Sean: I think it's a long shot, but definitely possible.

Sean：有可能，但是現在看起來機率不高。

UNIT 46

共識

▶▶影子跟讀「短對話」練習 MP3 046

此篇為**「影子跟讀短對話練習」**，此章節規劃了由聽**「短對話」**的shadowing練習，能從最基礎、最易上手的部分切入新多益聽力備考並提升考生的專注力，現在就一起動身，開始聽**「短對話」**！

Jennifer: So what exactly is difficult about working for your boss?

Jennifer：所以到底哪裡讓你覺得幫你老闆做事很困難？

Mark: We can never be on the same page, whatever I say he will always interpret the other way. It's driving me crazy!

Mark：我們從來沒辦法互相了解，他總是誤解我想要表達的意思。

Jennifer: That is strange. Did you try to talk to him about it?

Jennifer：喔！那真奇怪，你有試著跟他溝通過這件事嗎？

Mark: I tried, but there really is a communication problem between us. Do you think I can ask for a transfer?

Mark：有啊！但是我們中間就是有溝通上的問題，你覺得我有辦法申請調到別的部門嗎？

Jennifer: Yes, you always can, but it really depends on whether there is an opening in other divisions.

Jennifer：可以啊，可是那也要別的部門有空缺才行。

Mark: Thanks I will look into it.

Mark：謝謝，我會找找。

UNIT 46

共識

▶▶「短對話」填空練習 MP3 046

除了前面的**「影子跟讀短對話練習」**，現在試著在聽完對話後，完成下列對話中填空部分，從中強化生活場景中常見的字彙以及拼字能力，答案的話請參照前面的對話喔！

Jennifer: So what exactly is ________ about working for your boss?	**Jennifer**：所以到底哪裡讓你覺得幫你老闆做事很困難？
Mark: We can never be on the ________, whatever I say he will always ________ the other way. It's driving me ________!	**Mark**：我們從來沒辦法互相了解，他總是誤解我想要表達的意思。
Jennifer: That is ________. Did you try to talk to him about it?	**Jennifer**：喔！那真奇怪，你有試著跟他溝通過這件事嗎？

Mark: I tried, but there really is a __________ problem between us. Do you think I can ask for a __________?

Mark：有啊！但是我們中間就是有溝通上的問題，你覺得我有辦法申請調到別的部門嗎？

Jennifer: Yes, you __________ can, but it really __________ whether there is an __________ in other __________.

Jennifer：可以啊，可是那也要別的部門有空缺才行。

Mark: Thanks I will __________ it.

Mark：謝謝，我會找找。

Unit 1

停車場看出職場地位

Instructions

❶ 請播放音檔聽下列對話，並完成試題。MP3 047

1. What are the three people talking about?

(A) how to walk to the parking lot

(B) walking a lot is good for health

(C) the reason that they need to park far away from the building

(D) the reason that someone in a higher position parks farther from the building

2. Why do they need to park at D lot?

(A) because D lot is closer to the company

(B) because they are assistants

(C) because they want to walk a lot

(D) because it is free to park at D lot

3. Why does the man say, "I'm feeling a little better"?

(A) because those in higher positions also need to walk the same distance to the parking lot as he does

(B) because he feels walking to the parking lot makes him

more energetic
(C) because he enjoys the conversation with the woman
(D) because those in higher positions decided to give him a promotion

中譯與聽力原文

Questions 1-3 refer to the following conversation

James: Why do we have to park at D lot? It's five blocks away from the entrance building.

詹姆士： 為什麼我們要停在D停車場呢？離建築物入口要走五個街區。

Mary: Assistants park at D lot. That's the rule, unless you get promoted.

瑪　莉： 助理停在D停車場。這是規定，除非你獲得升遷。

James: Right, managers can park at B lot, two blocks away, and of course CEOs and clients, A lot.

詹姆士： 是啊，經理能停在B停車場，距離兩個街區遠，然後當然CEO和客戶停在A停車場。

Linda: You know what...what makes me feel better is that C lot and D lot are all five blocks away from the building, but

琳　達： 你知道嗎？...使我感到好多了的是C停車場和D停車場同樣都離建築物五個街區，

they are on the opposite of the company.

只是他們在公司相反的方位。

James: I'm feeling a little better, knowing someone who is in a superior position has to walk the same miles.

詹姆士：我覺得好些了，知道有些位階優於我們的工作者要走相同的路程。

選項中譯與解析

1. 兩人正在談論什麼？

(A) 如何走到停車場。

(B) 多走路有益健康。

(C) 他們需停離大樓很遠之處的原因。

(D) 某些高層人員，停在離大樓更遠處的原因。

2. 為何他們需要停在D停車場呢？

(A) 因為D停車場離公司更近。

(B) 因為他們是助理。

(C) 因為他們想要多走路。

(D) 因為停在D停車場是免費的。

3. 男子說「我覺得好些了」代表什麼意思？

(A) 因為那些位階優於他們的人也需要像他走相同的路程。

(B) 因為他覺得走到停車場讓他精力更充沛。

(C) 因為他喜歡和女子聊天。

(D) 因為那些位階較高的人決定讓他升遷。

1.

· 此題屬於情境題，題目詢問對話主要的討論內容，測試考生是否能理解對話內容。根據首句，我們可以得知對話內容是Why do we have to park at D lot?的延伸。因為D停車場距離入口較遠，而延伸出公司位階和升遷等討論。可以先刪除對話內容沒有提及的A、B選項，接著從C、D選項選出最符合答案的C選項：討論由於職位而必須停在D停車場的理由，可知**答案即為C**。

2.

· 此題屬於推測題，題目詢問他們停在D停車場的原因；關鍵字Assistant是助理的意思。根據對話，助理停在D停車場、經理停在B停車場、執行長和客戶停在A停車場；雖然主角沒有直接表明：we're assistants，但仍可以依此推測：他們停在D停車場的原因是因為**職位**。

3.

· **聽到對話，直接鎖定knowing someone who is in a superior position has to walk the same miles，直接解釋I'm feeling a little better的原因。**此題屬於推測題，測試考生是否能理解對話內容所提及的公司規定。根據對話，助理停在D停車場、經理停在B停車場、執行長和客戶停在A停車場；雖然沒有明確指出什麼職位的人停在C停車場，但我們可以推測C停車場的職位介於經理和助理的中間，也就是**高於助理的職位**。並且，C、D停車場距離公司都是五個街區遠，所以他才會說someone who is in a superior position has to walk the same miles：某些職位較高的人也和他們走相同的路程。

Unit 2

停 A 停車場，羨煞旁人

Instructions

❶ 請播放音檔聽下列對話，並完成試題。MP3 048

4. Why does the man say, “from now on I’ve got to work extra hard”?

(A) because he wants to make more money
(B) because the woman pushes him to work harder
(C) because he wants to get promoted
(D) because he wants to work out more

5. Why does the woman say, “Think of this as a transition”?

(A) Her company is experiencing a transitional period.
(B) She thinks their current status is temporary.
(C) She understands the man is going through some transitions.
(D) She sees that the man is experiencing personal transformation

6. Why does the man say, “I’m jealous”?

(A) He is jealous that some co-workers can park at Lot A.
(B) He is jealous that the woman has more clients.

(C) He envies the woman for her working capabilities

(D) He envies the woman because she walks faster than he does.

 中譯與聽力原文

Questions 4-6 refer to the following conversation

Mary: It's just temporary. We are all going to get promoted after three to five years. Think of this as a transition. Then you won't carry a negative mood into the work.

瑪　莉：這只是暫時的。我們總會在三到五年後升遷。想像一下這只是過渡期。然後你就不用在工作時帶著負面情緒。

Linda: I parked at A lot once. It was a great feeling, walking directly to the entrance. Five seconds. You can even do it in slow motion, still faster than anybody. A

琳　達：我有次停在A停車場。感覺很棒，直接走到路口。五秒。你甚至可以慢動作走到公司入口，卻仍比誰都快。

James: You've gotta to be kidding me, right? There is no way that you can park at A lot.

詹姆士：你在開玩笑對吧！你不可能可以停在A停車場。

Linda: Not if you're with managers

琳　達：如果你是跟著經理和

1 新多益基礎對話演練
2 新多益單篇對話和解析
3 新多益對話模擬試題

and major clients. 主要客戶的話就不在此限。

James: I'm jealous. It means from now on I've got to work extra hard.

詹姆士： 我忌妒了。這意味著從現在起我必須更努力工作。

選項中譯與解析

4. 男子說「從現在起我必須更努力工作」，代表何意？

(A) 因為他想賺更多的錢。

(B) 因為女子督促他更努力工作。

(C) 因為他想升遷。

(D) 因為他想多做運動。

5. 為何女子說「想像一下這只是過渡期」？

(A) 她公司正在經歷過渡期。

(B) 她認為目前的情況是暫時的。

(C) 她明白此人正在經歷某些轉變。

(D) 她看到此人正經歷個人轉變。

6. 為何男子說「我忌妒了」？

(A) 他忌妒一些同事可在A停車場停車。

(B) 他忌妒女子有更多的客戶。

(C) 他羨慕女子的工作能力。

(D) 他因為女子走得比他快而羨慕她。

4.

・根據對話，推測work extra hard的目的是為了**get promoted**，並藉由升遷，得到可以停在距離公司較近的停車場的資格。此題屬於推測題，需推測work extra hard的目的和結果，同時測驗考生是否理解get promoted的意思。根據對話，男士表示羨慕，是因為能停在距離公司較近的A停車場，而根據公司規定，除非升遷，否則助理必須停在D停車場；我們可以依此推測，男士表示要更努力工作是為了得到升遷，然後有機會可以停在距離公司較近的A、B停車場。

5.

・此題屬於情境題，測驗考生是否理解對話內容語意，同時測試考生關鍵字transition的字意。根據對話We are all going to get promoted after three to five years.可知女士認為他們三到五年後遲早會升遷，現狀只是暫時的過渡期。Transitional是形容詞：過渡的；transformation是名詞：轉型。我們可以先刪除錯誤的A、D選項，然後選出較符合敘述的B選項；C選項「她理解男士將會面臨一些過渡期」是一個干擾選項，並不是女士主要想表達的語意。

6.

・根據對話，It was a great feeling, walking directly to the entrance. ....可以推測停在A停車場是讓人羨慕的。此題屬於推測題，若無法推測答案，也可以將選項對照對話內容作刪去法。根據對話內容，沒有提到女士擁有較多客戶或是較高的工作能力，故B、C選項可以先做刪去；而女士之所以可以走得比別人快，是因為停在距離公司較近的A停車場；故**A選項**是最適合的答案。

Unit 3

提案會議真的沒這麼簡單

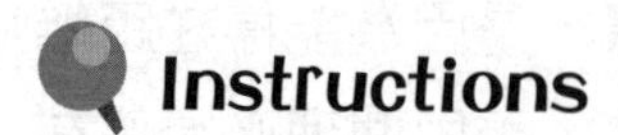

Instructions

❶ 請播放音檔聽下列對話，並完成試題。MP3 049

7. Where might the speakers be?

(A) on the beach
(B) in a zoo
(C) in a meeting room
(D) in an aquarium

8. What are they talking about?

(A) the environmentalists
(B) marine creatures
(C) their favorite stories
(D) the topic of a project

9. Why does the man say, "we will upload videos on Facebook"?

(A) The hits on the videos on Facebook will bring revenues.
(B) The hits on the videos will make him famous.
(C) He likes to make friends on Facebook by sharing videos.
(D) He believes sharing videos can raise the awareness of protecting dolphins.

中譯與聽力原文

Questions 7-9 refer to the following conversation

Jane: OK...Let's begin our pitch meeting as usual...Best Circus needs a feature story to rebuild its brand images, and the deadline is tomorrow...what do you have for me, team D?

簡：好的...讓我們像往常一樣開始我們的提案會議...倍斯特馬戲團需要一則能重建其品牌形象的專題故事，截止日期是明天...D團隊你們準備了什麼給我呢?

Mary: We're thinking about using dolphins as our feature story.

瑪莉：我們正考慮使用海豚當我們的專題故事。

Jimmy: You know how environmentalists love marine creatures. Dolphins are a good way for viewers to relate. Videos with interactions between visitors and dolphins can dilute the harm it has done before. Plus, we will upload videos on Facebook. Sharing videos can create hits, which will bring ad revenues.

吉米：你知道環境保護人士有多愛海洋生物。海豚是很容易讓觀看者有共鳴的生物。參觀者和海豚互動的視頻能夠減低先前所造成的傷害。再者，我們會上傳視頻到臉書。分享視頻能創造點擊率，這也會帶來廣告收益。

Jane: I think they are gonna love it.

簡：我覺得他們會很喜愛這個。

選項中譯與解析

7. 談話者目前身處哪裡？

(A) 在海灘。

(B) 在動物園。

(C) 在會議室。

(D) 在水族館。

8. 他們談論內容為何？

(A) 環保主義者。

(B) 海洋生物。

(C) 他們最喜愛的故事。

(D) 提案主題。

9. 為何男子說「我們會上傳影片到臉書」？

(A) 臉書上視頻的點擊率將帶來收益。

(B) 視頻的點擊率將使他成名。

(C) 他喜歡透過在臉書分享視頻來交友。

(D) 他認為分享視頻能提高保護海豚的意識。

7.

・根據對話內容，主要是一個環保相關的提案討論，可以推測討論人應處於會議中，故答案為C會議室。此題屬於細節題，考生須從對話細節中找出關鍵字，並依此推論答案。根據對話的關鍵字pitch meeting來延伸，team D以海豚為主軸設定了專案，可以推測討論應該是發生在會議室裡，除了D小組也還可能有其他組別和提案，但無法確定其他提案主題都跟環保或海洋生態有關，所以會議室是最適合的答案。

8.

・根據對話，討論內容由pitch meeting做延伸，圍繞著海洋環境保護做主題，可以推測討論內容為提案的主題，故**選項D**為最適合的答案。此題屬於情境題，測驗考生是否理解對話情境和對話內容，並依此推論答案。我們可以將8題視為7題的延伸，先確定了對話是會議中的提案討論，就可以直接確定選項D：企劃的主題是正確答案。A、B選項的環保人士和海洋生物在對話中都有出現，是誘答選項但不是討論的中心，要特別小心。

9.

・根據對話，Sharing videos can create hits, which will bring ads revenues.可知影片透過網路分享可以達到宣傳效益，故此題答案為**A**。此題屬於細節題，可以先鎖定題目句來定位問題點，再用刪去法找出答案。根據對話，Sharing videos can create hits, which will bring ads revenues.可知答案即為選項A；revenue是名詞「收入」，在此有「廣告效益」的意思。我們也可以先刪除對話未提及的B、C選項，接著從A、D選項選出最佳答案；由D選項的「sharing videos」來看，**語意偏向「分享影片」這個動作**，可以提高保護海豚的意識，但是沒有專指「分享提案的影片」，所以是一個有瑕疵的選項，不是最好的答案。

Unit 4

不厚臉皮可能就要丟飯碗了

Instructions

❶ 請播放音檔聽下列對話，並完成試題。MP3 050

10. Who are these men?

(A) car mechanics

(B) car salesmen

(C) car manufacturers

(D) car marketing specialists

11. Why did the man become Mary's assistant?

(A) Mary asked him to be her assistant.

(B) He volunteered to be Mary's assistant.

(C) He needs to learn from Mary's working performance.

(D) He likes to assist his co-workers.

12. Which of the following is the best description of Mary?

(A) Mary is the most experienced worker in this company.

(B) Mary always has the most clients.

(C) Mary is a new employee.

(D) Mary is good at selling cars.

中譯與聽力原文

Questions 10-12 refer to the following conversation

Jack: How many times do I have to tell you that you really need to develop a thick skin. You just have to let go of that rejection. I can't run those reports. It's zero.

傑克：我告訴你多少次你真的需要厚臉皮。你就是要放掉被拒絕的感覺。我無法看那些報告。銷售數字是零。

Jim: I totally understand. I'm working on it. Pretty soon it'll turn out to be ok.

吉姆：我完全能理解。我在努力了。很快事情都會沒問題的。

Jack: OK? You have been here for like...three months, but you haven't sold a car.

傑克：沒問題？你已經來這裡有...三個月了，但你尚未賣掉一台車。

Jack: From now on, I'm assigning you to watch how other people perform. You're now an assistant to Mary. She just won Employee of the Month Award. I'm sure she will tell you what to do. She always knows what she is doing.

傑克：從現在開始，我將你分派到觀看其他人如何銷售。你現在是瑪莉的助理。她剛贏得每月最佳員工獎。我相信她會告訴你怎麼做。她總是知道自己在做什麼。

選項中譯與解析

10. 這些人的職業為何？

(A) 汽車修理員。

(B) 汽車業務。

(C) 汽車製造商。

(D) 汽車經銷專家。

11. 男子成為瑪麗助理的原因為何？

(A) 瑪麗讓他當助理。

(B) 他自願成為瑪麗的助理。

(C) 他需要向瑪麗學習工作方面的表現。

(D) 他喜歡幫助同事。

12. 下列關於瑪麗的描述，何者最佳？

(A) 瑪麗是這間公司最有經驗的員工。

(B) 瑪麗擁有的客戶一直最多。

(C) 瑪麗是一名新進員工。

(D) 瑪麗擅長賣車。

10.

・此題屬於情境題，測試考生是否能抓出對話中的關鍵字，並理解對話情境。根據對話，從develop a thick skin、let go of that rejection還有最關鍵的you haven't sold a car，可以推測他們的工作跟銷售、推銷最有關係。(A)car mechanics指的是負責維修保養的汽車機械師；(C)car manufacturers指的是汽車製造廠商；(D)car marketing specialists指的是負責市場評估、定位等等的汽車營銷專家。

11.

・根據對話前後句，watch how other people perform、she will tell you what to do，可知他擔任Mary的助理是為了學習銷售技巧。此題屬於推測題，考生須根據對話情境和內容推測答案，也可搭配刪去法解題。11題可以作為10題的延伸，先確定了此人的身分是汽車的銷售員，接著由題目you haven't sold a car.、I'm assigning you to watch how other people perform.可以推測此人是因為銷售成績太差，所以先被任命為Mary的助理，進而從旁觀察和學習別人的銷售技巧，故此題答案為**選項C**。

12.

・根據對話watch how other people perform，來推測Mary是很有銷售技巧並值得學習的，所以選項D是最適合的答案。此題屬於細節題，考生須根據選項一一回推比照對話細節，選出最正確的選項。根據對話，She just won Employee of the Month Award.、She always knows what she is doing.可知Mary剛獲選為本月的最佳員工、她的工作表現很好；我們可以先刪除無法由對話判斷是否正確的A、C選項，再從B、D選項選出答案。根據對話，我們可以推測Mary是很有銷售技巧並值得學習的，但是無法確定她總是有最多的顧客，所以B也是一個有瑕疵的選項，故此題**答案為D**。

Unit 5

漏了要做員工識別證

Instructions

❶ 請播放音檔聽下列對話，並完成試題。MP3 051

13. How many new badges do they need to make?

(A) 10

(B) 20

(C) 5

(D) 15

14. What does the woman mean by saying, “I have no errands to run?

(A) She needs to move faster to deal with some business.

(B) She is bored with running errands.

(C) Running can boost her working performance.

(D) She has no business to attend to at this moment.

15. Who are these speakers?

(A) colleagues

(B) new employees

(C) new recruits

(D) Cindy’s friends

中譯與聽力原文

Questions 13-15 refer to the following conversation

Linda: Cindy forgot to prepare new ID badges for our new hires. I can't believe this is happening.

琳達：辛蒂忘了替我們錄取新人準備新的識別證。我不敢相信這件事發生了。

Jane: How many? I thought she did this yesterday.

簡：多少？我以為她昨天完成了。

Linda: Ten to be exact, but I have to prepare documents for the HR managers; there is no way that I can make the new ID badges now.

琳達：準確來說是十個，但是我必須準備給人事經理們的文件，我現在不可能有時間做新的識別證。

Jack: I saw her at the gate, leading new recruits to the hall.

傑克：我在大門看到她，帶領新人們到大廳。

Jane: Yesterday was so chaotic. Perhaps I can make new ID badges for her. I have no errands to run. If they're ten new badges short, this can be done by noon. Ten new ID

簡：昨天太忙亂了。或許我可以幫她做新的識別證。我沒有差事。如果短少10個新的識別證，那中午前我可以完成。十個新的識別證通常要花費兩小時。

badges usually take around two hours.

Jack: I was just on the phone with an HR manager. It's twenty.

傑克：我剛跟人事部經理在電話中確認過了。是20個。

選項中譯與解析

13. 他們需要多少新的識別證？

(A) 10
(B) 20
(C) 5
(D) 15

14. 女子說「我沒有差事」，這句話意思為何？

(A) 她需趕快去處理業務。
(B) 她厭倦了差事。
(C) 跑步可以提高她的工作表現。
(D) 她現在沒什麼需要處理的事。

15. 這些談話者是誰？

(A) 同事。
(B) 新員工。
(C) 新成員。
(D) 辛蒂的朋友。

13.

・badge是名詞徽章、證章的意思，此處的ID badges 指的是員工的識別證。根據對話I was just on the phone with an HR manager. It's twenty.可知正確數量是20個，故此題**答案為B**。此題屬於細節題，考生須透過對話細節了解對話情境，並推測答案。根據對話，Cindy forgot to prepare new ID badges for our new hires.可知目前所需的識別證數量是新進員工的數量，從Ten to be exact到It's twenty.，可知A選項是一個**誘答選項**，正確數字為20個。

14.

・Errand是名詞：差事、雜事的意思，一般搭配動詞run使用，所以have no errands to run就是沒有差事要忙，故此題**答案為D**。此題屬於細節題及推測題，考生須先理解動詞片語have no errands to run的意思，對照選項找出意思類似的片語，並推測出答案。根據對話，have no errands to run和D選項has no business to attend to意思相近，attend to是動詞片語，處理之意，搭配對話Perhaps I can make new ID badges for her，可以推測此人目前沒有事情要忙，所以可以幫忙，故D選項是最符合的答案。

15.

・根據對話，從new hires、new recruits和HR manager彼此的關係來推測，說話者最有可能是公司同事，負責處理新進人員的人事資料。此題屬於情境題，測試考生是否理解對話情境並判斷人物關係。根據對話prepare new ID badges for our new hires可知說話者並不是新進員工，即可先刪除錯誤的B、C選項。由於無法從對話明確得知說話只和Cindy是不是朋友，所以A選項「同事」是最適合的答案。

Unit 6 員工識別證換餐點，水果 = 糖份

Instructions

❶ 請播放音檔聽下列對話，並完成試題。 MP3 052

16. Why did Mark give the man his ID badge?

(A) because Mark became sick and did not need to use his badge in the company cafeteria

(B) because Mark and the man are best friends

(C) because Mark does not like to eat in the company cafeteria

(D) because Mark asked the man to buy some food for him from the company cafeteria

17. Why did the man get only fruits?

(A) His favorite food is fruit.

(B) Fruits are on sale.

(C) He wants to ingest more Vitamin C from fruits.

(D) He is watching his weight

18. Why does the man say, "if I were Jim, I would be more concerned with sugar in those fruits"?

(A) He does not like to eat sweet food.

(B) He knows that Jim does not like sweet fruits.

(C) He thinks Jim should be worried about the lack of sugar in those fruits.

(D) He thinks Jim should pay attention to the amount of sugar in so many kinds of fruits.

 中譯與聽力原文

Questions 16-18 refer to the following conversation

Jack: How can you get so many fruits at the company cafeteria?

傑克：你怎麼能從公司自助餐廳拿那麼多水果呢？

Jim: Mark had a sick leave this afternoon, and he had given me his ID badge before he left, and since I'm sort of on a diet...so all the fruits.

吉姆：馬克今天下午請病假，而且在他離開公司前，他給我他的識別證，而且既然我有點再節食...所以都是水果。

Jack: Let me get this straight. For each badge, it's 150 NT dollars per meal, which means you just bought yourself fruits worthy of 300 NT dollars.

傑克：讓我埋清頭緒。每個識別證每餐可使用金額是150元台幣。所以你剛替自己買了價值300元台幣的水果。

Jim: Yep...bananas, grapefruits, apples, and kiwi.

吉姆：是的...香蕉、葡萄、蘋果和奇異果。

Mary: Still trying hard to figure out the fruit mania thing. But is that legal?

瑪莉：仍試著了解整個水果狂熱事。但是這合法嗎？

Jack: It's not something for us to decide, but if I were Jim, I would be more concerned with sugar in those fruits.

傑克：這不是由我們來決定，但如果我是吉姆，我會更在乎那些水果中的糖分。

選項中譯與解析

16. 為什麼馬克把識別證交給男子？

(A) 因為馬克生病了，他不需要在員工餐廳使用識別證。

(B) 因為馬克和那男子是最好的朋友。

(C) 因為馬克不喜歡在員工餐廳吃飯。

(D) 因為馬克要求此人到員工餐廳替他買些食物。

17. 為何此男子只拿水果？

(A) 他最喜歡的食物是水果。

(B) 水果正在特價。

(C) 他想從水果攝取更多的維生素C.

(D) 他正在節食。

18. 為何此男子說「如果我是吉姆，我會更在乎那些水果中的糖分」？

(A) 他不喜歡吃甜食。

(B) 他知道吉姆不喜歡甜的水果。

(C) 他認為吉姆應該擔心那些水果中缺乏糖分。

(D) 他認為吉姆應該注意這麼多種水果中的含糖量。

16.

・sick leave是名詞「病假」的意思，根據對話可知Mark下午病假，可以推測他不會在公司用餐，故此題**答案為A**。此題屬於細節題，此處的ID badge，指的是身分的識別證。可以先鎖定關鍵字sick leave來推測Mark今天由於生病請假，不會在員工餐廳用餐所以不需要他的識別證；接著用刪去法，刪除對話內容無法得知的B、C、D選項，確定A選項為最適合的答案。

17.

・on a diet是片語表示「節食」、「減肥」的意思，可以推測此人正在控制體重，故答案為**選項D**。此題屬於細節題，考生須先了解動詞片語be on a diet的用法，然後推測此人只選擇水果的原因。從be on a diet 找到他的類似用法「watch one's weight」，兩者都有控制體重的意思。根據對話，此人將重點放在節食，並沒有提及喜歡水果或是水果的其他好處，也可以用刪去法得到正解。

18.

・根據對話，you just bought yourself fruits worthy of 300 NT dollars.可知他的午餐是大量的水果，對於在節食的人來說，也可能會攝取過多的糖分。此題屬於推測題，根據對話細節推測語意，可以搭配刪去法解題。根據對話關鍵字「on a diet」，可知正在節食的Jim企圖以大量的水果取代正餐，我們可以推測說話者認為sugar in those fruits將無益於正在節食的Jim，所以需要特別留意水果中的糖分。對話中的be concerned with「關心」、「關注於」是D選項pay attention to的同義詞。

Unit 7

情人節：巧克力盒看人生

Instructions

❶ 請播放音檔聽下列對話，並完成試題。MP3 053

19. What holiday are they talking about?

(A) Christmas

(B) Thanksgiving

(C) Valentine's Day

(D) Easter

20. How do the speakers feel about getting bouquets and chocolates?

(A) sad

(B) frustrated

(C) cheerful

(D) uncertain

21. What does the sentence "Life is like a box of chocolate" imply?

(A) We cannot predict what will happen to us.

(B) We should eat more chocolates.

(C) Chocolates are good for our health.

(D) Life is bitter sweet, just like chocolate.

中譯與聽力原文

Questions 19-21 refer to the following conversation

Cindy: So considerate. Everyone gets a bouquet and a box of chocolate on Valentine's Day. The box totally makes my day, so fancy.

辛蒂： 真是體貼入微。在情人節，每個人都收到花束和一盒巧克力。今天全然因為這盒而讓人感到美好，很豪華。

Mandy: Yep, kind of sweet. I love this company. You won't have a feeling that you are desperately lonely. There is no way that your colleague gets a boutique from an admirer, but you don't.

曼蒂： 是的，有點體貼。我喜愛這間公司。你不用有種你本身極度寂寞。也不會有著你同事收到愛慕著的花束，但你卻沒收到。

Cindy: Those feelings...even if it sounds like so tiny, it actually affects how we're going to perform at work.

辛蒂： 那些感覺...即使看起來很些微，實際上卻影響我們在工作上如何表現。

Mandy: I'm gonna go with the strawberry flavor...Eww it tastes bitter.

曼蒂： 我要先嚐草莓口味的...哎喲...嚐起來苦。

Jim: It's like life. Life is like a box of chocolates; you don't know what it is until you experience it.

吉姆：就像生命一樣。人生像是一盒巧克力，你不知道會是什麼直到你體驗了。

選項中譯與解析

19. 他們在談論什麼節日？

(A) 聖誕節。

(B) 感恩節。

(C) 情人節。

(D) 復活節。

20. 說話者對花束和巧克力看法如何？

(A) 難過的。

(B) 挫折的。

(C) 開心的。

(D) 不確定的。

21. 「人生像是一盒巧克力」，這句話含意為何？

(A) 我們無法預測我們會發生什麼事。

(B) 我們應該多吃巧克力。

(C) 巧克力有益健康。

(D) 生活苦樂參半，就像巧克力一樣。

19.

· **聽到對話，馬上鎖定關鍵字Valentine's Day**，可知對話談論的是情人節。配合對話gets a bouquet and a box of chocolate等內容，最符合情人節的送禮項目，故此題**答案為C**。此題屬於情境題，可以直接鎖定對話關鍵字Valentine's Day，接著透過對話中的bouquet、a box of chocolate和gets a boutique from an admirer等細節來驗證，最符合這樣的節日就是情人節，所以答案即為C。

1 新多益基礎對話演練
2 新多益單篇對話和解析
3 新多益對話模擬試題

20.

・根據對話，How sweet is that、makes my day、so fancy等感嘆語和形容詞，可知收到花束和巧克力是讓人感到十分貼心和雀躍的。此題屬於細節題及推測題，考生須先理解慣用語make one's day的意思，接著推測與make one's day相關的情緒形容詞。片語make one's day有讓人非常開心的意思，就像讓人的一天都因此而美好，搭配對話中提到的sweet、fancy，都有很正向的意思，所以與其最相近的就是選項**(C)cheerful快樂的**。

21.

・需特別留意結論句you don't know what it is until you experience it.由此可知，人生像一盒巧克力，是因為必須品嚐了才知道滋味，故此題**答案為A**。此題屬於推測題，考生須根據題目細節推測答案，可以搭配選項的刪去法來解答。Life is like a box of chocolate，是比喻的句型。又根據對話關鍵句：you don't know what it is until you experience it「必須經歷才能理解」來對照選項，可知選項A的內容「人生是無法預測的」和題目意義最為相近。也可先刪除錯誤的B、C選項；而**D選項「人生有苦有甜」是一個誘答選項要特別小心**。

Unit 8

慶幸自己是會計部門的人

Instructions

❶ 請播放音檔聽下列對話，並完成試題。 MP3 054

22. What are the speakers discussing?

(A) the issue at the pitch meeting

(B) the issue of reducing expenses in the company

(C) how to make the boss satisfied

(D) working in the accounting department

23. How might the woman feel at the pitch meeting?

(A) frustrated

(B) pleased

(C) excited

(D) sad

24. Which of the following is the closest in meaning to the word "pitch" in this conversation?

(A) the level of something

(B) a proposal that attempts to persuade someone

(C) a throw in a baseball game

(D) the tone of a voice

中譯與聽力原文

Questions 22-24 refer to the following conversation

Mary: I just don't understand what our CFO said at the budget meeting. Are we short of money?

瑪莉： 我就是無法了解我們財務長在預算會議說的話。我們資金短缺嗎？

Jack: I think we are. They're cutting expenses on almost everything.

傑克： 我想我們是。他們現在幾乎每件事都在砍支出。

Jane: No wonder, I'm having a feeling that I'm having a hard time at the pitch meeting as well. For the past two months, none. The boss is never gonna be satisfied with any pitch.

簡： 難怪，我有種感覺，我在提案會議時感到很難通過。過去兩個月，通過0個。老闆幾乎不滿意任何提案。

Mary: Thank God! I'm from Accounting Department.

瑪莉： 謝天謝地！我是會計部門的。

Jack: Why don't you go with the "it's gonna save lots of money", or "cost cutting", instead of focusing on the idea?

傑克： 為什麼我們不走「這會省許多錢」或「減少支出」而不是重心放在點子上呢？

Mary: Perhaps, they're looking for a pitch that will cost the least money, but can earn lots of money in the long run. They don't care about which topic you pitch as long as they are feeling it's costly.

瑪莉：或許，他們正找尋會花費最少錢的提案，但是最終卻能賺許多錢。他們不在乎你所提的提案，只要他們覺得很花錢。

選項中譯與解析

22. 談話者正在討論什麼？

(A) 提案會議上的問題。

(B) 公司減少開支的問題。

(C) 如何讓老闆滿意。

(D) 在會計部門工作。

23. 女子在開提案會議時可能的感覺為何？

(A) 沮喪的。

(B) 高興的。

(C) 興奮的。

(D) 難過的。

24. 本篇談話中，下列何者和pitch 的意思最接近？

(A) 事情程度。

(B) 試圖說服某人的提案。

(C) 棒球比賽的投球。

(D) 音調。

22.

・根據對話，short of money跟cutting expenses，可知討論主題是關於公司的預算縮減，故此題**答案為B**。此題為情境題，根據對話，從Are we short of money?開啟話題，接著提到They're cutting expenses on almost everything.，可知對話主題圍繞著公司預算縮減的事件，與B選項reducing expenses意思最相近，故答案為B。

23.

・根據對話I'm having a hard time at the pitch meeting、The boss is never gonna be satisfied with any pitch.可以推測此人在提案會議中感到挫折。此題為細節題，考生須先了解關鍵的動詞片語have a hard time的意思，對照選項找出意思最相近的詞。have a hard time是「有一段艱難的時光」的意思，根據對話The boss is never gonna be satisfied with any pitch.可以推測選項(A) frustrated「挫折的」是最相近的詞，故此題**答案為A**。

24.

・此處的pitch指的是提案，pitch meeting也就是提案會議。根據關鍵字的相關敘述，satisfied with any pitch、focusing on the idea 和which topic you pitch等來推測，pitch指的是想法、主題的提案。此題為細節題，可以根據對話satisfied with any pitch.、focusing on the idea、looking for a pitch和which topic you pitch等細節，推測pitch和B選項的proposal 最為相近，故此題**答案為B**：嘗試說服某人的提案。

Unit 9

不靠大量訂單也談成某個折扣

Unit 9 大標

Instructions

❶ 請播放音檔聽下列對話，並完成試題。MP3 055

25. What does the woman mean by saying "Isn't that wild"?

(A) Mr. Smith is a wild person.

(B) A huge discount is pretty amazing.

(C) Talking on the phone about the order makes her angry.

(D) It is not reasonable to place a bulk order.

26. How would they receive a discount under normal circumstances?

(A) by placing a bulk order

(B) by negotiating with Mr. Smith

(C) by doing something under the table

(D) by bargaining with Mr. Smith

27. Why does the woman say, "I guess that will be my little secret"?

(A) She is good at keeping secrets.

(B) The order is confidential information.

(C) Mr. Smith asked her to keep a secret.

(D) She does not want to reveal how she received the discount.

中譯與聽力原文

Questions 25-27 refer to the following conversation

Jane: I was just on the phone with Mr. Smith, and he said that he would give us a huge discount at our CY10008 order. Isn't that wild?

簡：我剛才與史密斯先生通話，他說CY10008的訂單他會給我大量折扣。是不是很瘋狂？

Jack: Congratulations. Normally, he won't give us a discount, unless it's a bulk order.

傑克：恭喜。通常，他不會給我們折扣，除非這是大量訂單。

Mark: Meaning we have to order a certain amount to have a discount?

馬克：意思是我們必須訂購到特定的量才能享有折扣嗎？

Jack: Yep. Just a little bit curious how you can pull that off.

傑克：是的。只是有點好奇你怎麼能成功做到。

Mark: How? I'm curious about that, too.

馬克：怎麼辦到的呢？我也蠻好奇的。

Jane: I guess that will be my little secret. Oh...the boss wants to see me. I'm gonna see you guys later.

簡：我想那就成了我的小秘密了。喔...老闆想要見我。我稍後再與你們見面。

選項中譯與解析

25. 女子說「是不是很瘋狂」含意為何？

(A) 史密斯先生是個狂人。

(B) 大量的折扣相當驚喜的。

(C) 在電話中談論訂單讓她生氣。

(D) 大量訂單是不合理的。

26. 在正常情況下，他們想獲得折扣該如何做呢？

(A) 透過大量訂購。

(B) 與史密斯先生協商。

(C) 私下交易。

(D) 與史密斯先生討價還價。

27. 為何女子說「我想那就成了我的小秘密」？

(A) 她善於保密。

(B) 訂單是機密資訊。

(C) 史密斯先生要求她保守秘密。

(D) 她不想透露如何得到折扣。

25.

・根據對話，he said that he could give us a huge discount，可知此人感到wild的原因跟得到大量折扣有關，故此題**答案為B**。此題屬於情境題，根據對話，Normally, he won't give us a discount, unless it's a bulk order.「可知除非是大量訂單，否則一般很難有辦法拿到折扣」，由此推測此處的Isn't that wild是想表達對於拿到大量折扣感到驚喜，所以最適合的答案為B。

26.

・根據對話，Normally, he won't give us a discount, unless it's a bulk order.，可知通常是透過大量訂單取得折扣的，故此題**答案為A**。此題為細節題，題目關鍵在under normal circumstances，考生可以從題目回推到對話，對照對話中的「Normally」找到關鍵字bulk order。根據對話Normally, he won't give us a discount, unless it's a bulk order.很明確的表示通常常是透過大量訂單拿到折扣，底下也解釋必須order a certain amount to have a discount，故此題答案為A。

27.

・根據對話，I guess that will be my little secret.表示說話者對於取得折扣的方法想要保密，故此題**答案為D**。此題屬於推測題，根據對話，Normally, he won't give us a discount, unless it's a bulk order.，可知這次能取得大量折扣，有別於一般狀況，而從I guess that will be my little secret.來推測說話者並不想公開方法，故答案為(D)She does not want to reveal how she received the discount.。

Unit 10
有人挖角，其他事都要讓道

Instructions

❶ 請播放音檔聽下列對話，並完成試題。MP3 056

28. Why is the woman not in the annual budget meeting?

(A) She is not well prepared for the meeting.
(B) She cannot make it on time.
(C) The meeting was rescheduled to tomorrow.
(D) The meeting was called off.

29. Why does the woman say, "I'm afraid not"?

(A) She is afraid to attend the budget meeting.
(B) She is not afraid to apply for a position in G&XM.
(C) She is unable to go through some reports.
(D) She is unable to talk to the shareholders.

30. When might the woman help with the reports conducted by Accounting Department?

(A) tomorrow afternoon
(B) tomorrow morning
(C) this evening
(D) right after they finish the conversation

中譯與聽力原文

Questions 28-30 refer to the following conversation

Mark: Why are you still here? Don't you have an annual budget meeting with bosses and shareholders?	**馬克：**為什麼你仍在這裡？你不是與老闆們和股東們有個年度預算會議嗎？
Jane: They rescheduled it to tomorrow morning yesterday.	**簡：**昨天他們將它重新安排至明天早上。
Mary: That means you'll have time to go through the reports conducted by the Accounting Department, right?	**瑪莉：**這意味著你將有時間看完由會計部門的報告，對吧？
Jane: I'm afraid not. G&XM just called. They're going to offer me a job. Isn't that wild? The interview is in the afternoon at 3 p.m. I've got some paper work to prepare. I do have time tomorrow afternoon. Don't worry about those reports. Gotta run.	**簡：**恐怕不能。G&XM剛來電。他們要提供我一份工作。是不是很瘋狂？面試是下午三點鐘。我有些文件資料要準備。我明天下午有時間。別擔心那些報告。該走囉。

選項中譯與解析

28. 為何女子不參加年度預算會議？

(A) 她沒有做好準備。

(B) 她不能按時完成。

(C) 重新安排至明天。

(D) 會議被取消了。

29. 為何女子說「恐怕不能」？

(A) 她怕參加預算會議。

(B) 她不怕在G＆XM申請工作。

(C) 她看不完一些報告。

(D) 她不能和股東交談。

30. 女子什麼時候可以幫會計部門處理報告？

(A) 明天下午。

(B) 明天早上。

(C) 今天晚上。

(D) 對話結束後。

28.

・根據對話，They rescheduled it to tomorrow morning yesterday. 可知會議被改期至明天早上，故此題**答案為C**。此題為細節題，測試考生是否理解對話內容，可以對照選項，配合刪去法解題。根據對話，They rescheduled it to tomorrow morning yesterday.可知答案為C選項：The meeting was rescheduled to tomorrow.：reschedule，動詞「改期」。(A) 她沒有準備好；(B)她趕不上；(D)會

議取消了。

29.

・根據上一句That means you'll have time to go through the reports conducted by Accounting Department, right?。但此人回答的是：I'm afraid I don't have time to go through the reports.，表達婉轉拒絕對方的要求，故**答案為C**。此題為細節題及推測題，根據對話問答，轉折句I'm afraid not是針對「have time to go through the reports conducted by Accounting Department」的否定，接著她馬上解釋否定的原因：G&XM just called. They're going to offer me a job. ... I've got some paper work to prepare，所以此人沒辦法看完會計部的報告，故此題答案為C。

30.

・根據對話，I do have time tomorrow afternoon.可知他明天下午有空，故此題**答案為A**。此題為細節題，題目關鍵在於the reports conducted by Accounting Department；也可視為29題的延伸，測試考生是否知道此人目前無法讀完的會計報告，會在什麼時候讀完。根據對話， The interview is in the afternoon 3 p.m. I've got some paper works to prepare.，可知她今天下午3點前要準備資料，然後3點開始面試；但是I do have time tomorrow afternoon. Don't worry about those reports.可知她明天下午有空。

Unit 11

家庭跟工作只能二選一

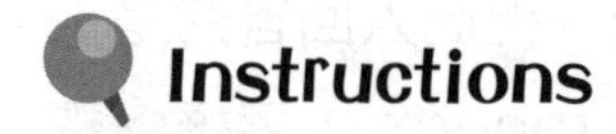

Instructions

❶ 請播放音檔聽下列對話，並完成試題。MP3 057

31. Why does the woman say, "it's a long fall from the top"?

(A) The sales figures fell to a very low number.

(B) She is telling the others to be careful not to fall.

(C) She feels the fall season is too long.

(D) It's a long distance from the cafeteria to the meeting room.

32. Why does the woman ask everyone to grab a bagel or sandwich?

(A) Bagels and sandwiches are their favorite.

(B) She expects everyone to attend the meeting and have dinner there.

(C) The cafeteria is known for its bagels and sandwiches.

(D) She does not want her co-workers to eat at the cafeteria.

33. What is the purpose of mentioning a family obligation by one of the women?

(A) to show a family obligation should be a priority.

(B) to indicate that family should come first

(C) She is suggesting that she cannot attend the meeting because of family duty.

(D) She is telling the co-workers that family duty is more important than meetings.

中譯與聽力原文

Questions 31-33 refer to the following conversation

Mary:	It's totally unacceptable...it's a long fall from the top.	**瑪莉：**	這全然令人無法接受...從頂端跌至最底。
Jack:	We've seen those sales figures. We're going to reposition our market place. Plus. We are launching a new feature next month. I'm pretty confident that we are gonna get back on track.	**傑克：**	我們已經看了銷售數字。我們正重新定位我們的市場位置。再者，我們下個月會推出一個新的專題。我相當有信心我們會回到正軌的。
Mary:	I want everyone to grab a bagel or sandwich at the cafeteria and meet back here at 6 p.m.	**瑪莉：**	我要求每個人到自助餐拿個貝果或三明治然後下午六點在這裡會合。
Judy:	I'm sorry. I've got a family obligation.	**茱蒂：**	很抱歉。我有家庭義務要履行。

Mary: Excuse me? This is an important sales meeting. If the condition hasn't improved, a lot of you might as well have to dust off your resume and find another job.

瑪莉： 不好意思？這是很重要的銷售會議。如果情況尚未改善的話，你們很多人都必須更新履歷另外找工作了。

選項中譯與解析

31.為何女子說「從頂端跌至最底」？

(A) 銷售數字下跌到很低的數字。

(B) 她正告訴別人小心不要跌倒。

(C) 她覺得秋天太長了。

(D) 從自助餐廳到會議室距離很遠。

32.為何女子要求大家拿個貝果或三明治？

(A) 貝果和三明治是他們的最愛。

(B) 她希望每個人都出席會議並在那吃晚餐。

(C) 自助餐廳以焙果和三明治而聞名。

(D) 她不希望同事在自助餐廳吃東西。

33.其中一名女子提到家庭義務，其目的為何？

(A) 表示家庭義務應該要優先考慮。

(B) 表示家庭應優先考慮。

(C) 她暗示因家家庭義務而不能出席會議。

(D) 她告訴同事，家庭義務比會議更重要。

31.

・找出關鍵字sales figures。 sales figures指的是銷售數字；根據對話，We've seen those sales figures.可以推測這裡的long fall from the top是針對sales figures，故此題**答案A**。此題屬於情境題及推測題，測試考生是否理解對話內容和討論主題，從而推測It's a long fall的指涉對象，也可由對話細節對照選項，配合刪去法解答。根據對話，從it's a long fall from the top到we are gonna get back from tack這幾句，可以確定long fall指涉的是對話主題字sales figures從頂端跌至最底的狀況，和A選項的敘述：「銷售數字下滑到非常嚴重」最為相近，故此題答案為A。

32.

・根據對話grab a bagel or sandwich at the cafeteria and meet back here和This is an important sales meeting.，可以推測她希望大家能一邊吃飯一邊開會。此題屬於情境題及推測題，根據對話This is an important sales meeting. If the condition hasn't improved, a lot of you might as well have to dust your resume and find another job.可知目前的情況十分嚴重，有可能影響員工生計，強調了這個會議很緊急也非常重要，可以推測此人是希望大家能一起吃飯、一邊開會討論對策，故**答案為B**。

33.

・Obligation是名詞「義務」。題目重點在於，詢問提起family obligation「家庭義務」的目的，推測此人有私人因素不便參加會議，故**答案為C**。此題屬於推測題，family obligation指的是家庭義務，與選項中的family duty同義。對照選項，A、B、D敘述內容大同小異，認為家庭比工作重要；C選項則強調無法參加會議，有請假的目的，最符合對話情境，故答案為C。

Unit 12
廣告收益幾乎決定公司生死

Instructions

❶ 請播放音檔聽下列對話，並完成試題。MP3 058

34. What are the speakers discussing?

(A) how awful the economy has become

(B) how to attract more sponsors

(C) how to stay positive

(D) how to increase earnings for the magazine

35. What is a possible solution to their problem?

(A) by marketing the magazine on social media

(B) by staying positive about the future

(C) by reducing the employees' salaries

(D) by doing business with ABC company

36. What does the woman imply by saying "The economy has hit us all"?

(A) The economy will be better.

(B) She could not believe how devastating the economy is.

(C) The economic recession has affected everyone.

(D) Generating hits on the magazine's Facebook page will bring more ad revenues.

中譯與聽力原文

Questions 34-36 refer to the following conversation

Jane: Did anyone call back?	**簡**：有任何人回電嗎？
Mark: no, why?	**馬克**：沒有，怎麼了？
Mary: The economy has hit us all. Apparently, no one wants to fund a magazine because they think that the magazine won't earn any money for them.	**瑪莉**：經濟不景氣衝擊到我們所有人。顯然沒有人想要注資雜誌，因為他們都認為雜誌不會替他們賺到錢。
Jane: Without ad revenues, there's no way we're gonna put our next issue on the stand.	**簡**：沒有廣告收入，我們不可能有辦法讓我們下期雜誌上架。
Mark: However, I do have a lunch meeting with ABC Company. I'm sure we'll find a way out.	**馬克**：然而，我與ABC公司有午餐會議。我確信我們會找到解決方法的。
Mary: We just have to be positive. I'm contacting our CFO to see if there are other things that we can do. We're gonna go through this.	**瑪莉**：我們就該抱持著正向思考。我正聯繫我們的財務長看是否有其他事情是我們所能做的。我們能撐過這個的。

選項中譯與解析

34. 談話者正在討論什麼？

(A) 經濟變得有多糟。

(B) 如何吸引更多贊助商。

(C) 如何保持正向。

(D) 如何增加雜誌的收入。

35. 可能解決問題的方案是什麼？

(A) 在社交媒體上行銷雜誌。

(B) 對未來保持樂觀。

(C) 減少員工薪水〔減薪〕。

(D) 與ABC公司做生意。

36. 女子對話中說「經濟不景氣衝擊到我們所有人」，其暗示為何？

(A) 經濟會更好。

(B) 她不敢相信經濟有多慘。

(C) 經濟不景氣已經影響到每個人。

(D) 雜誌臉書頁面的點擊量將帶來更多廣告收入。

34.

・根據對話，find a way out和go through this，判斷對話討論主題再找解決方案，所以**D選項**是最適合的答案。此題屬於情境題，測試考生是否理解對話主要內容，進而挑選出對話主題，也可對照選項，搭配刪去法解題。根據對話，從The economy has hit us all.開啟話題，提到目前雜誌的窘境，接著在轉折詞However之後提出可能解套的機會和動作；可以先刪除錯誤的A、C選項。對比B、D選項；B選項較片面的針對討論「如何尋找贊助商」，所以D選項的「想辦法增加收入」會是較好的答案。

35.

· 根據對話，I do have a lunch meeting with ABC Company. I'm sure we'll find a way out.，可知和ABC公司做生意有可能解決困境，故答案為D。此題屬於細節題，鎖定關鍵的轉折詞However，從困境轉折到可能的解決機會。根據對話，I do have a lunch meeting with ABC Company. I'm sure we'll find a way out.，find a way out表示「找到出路」，由此推測D選項doing business with ABC company會是解決問題的好機會，故此題**答案為D**。

36.

· 根據對話，The economy has hit us all.，關鍵字hit：動詞「打擊」，就字面解釋：經濟打擊所有人；可知答案即為**選項C**。此題屬於細節題及推測題，測試考生是否理解對話內容，運用換句話説，並通過對話細節對照選項，選出意思最接近The economy has hit us all的答案。根據對話內容，The economy has hit us all.以及雜誌面臨的危機，可以推測經濟帶來了不好的影響，最符合C選項「經濟蕭條影響所有人」的敘述，故答案為C。

▶ **PART 3** MP3 059

Directions: In this part, you will listen to several conversations between two or more speakers. These conversations will not be printed and will only be spoken one time. For each conversation, you will be asked to answer three questions. Select the best response and mark the corresponding letter (A), (B), (C), (D) on the answer sheet.

---

32. Where most likely is the conversation taking place?

(A) in a restaurant
(B) at a wine cellar
(C) in the kitchen
(D) on the airplane

---

33. What does the man recommend?

(A) take the complaint to the customer
(B) tell customers the truth
(C) do as instructed
(D) give customers more expensive wine

34. Why does the man say, "definitely not using what's holding in your hands"?

(A) to extinguish the fire
(B) to remind the woman
(C) to control the situation
(D) to cultivate the relationship

35.What industry do the speakers most likely work in?

(A) fire-fighting
(B) airline
(C) police
(D) safety training

36.What is the problem?

(A) the smoke is too heavy.
(B) using both hands to clear up the fog is not enough.
(C) the woman fails to do the task
(D) the woman shouldn't use the mask

37.Why does the woman say, "don't you think you are overreacting..."?

(A) she knows in advance that the examiner is going to overreact.
(B) she doesn't want the examiner to act like this way.
(C) she is pointing out the problem of the examiner.
(D) she is being dramatic about how the examiner said about her.

38.What is the problem?

(A) the shipment of the flowers will be postponed.
(B) the artificial setting for the flower is malfunctioned.
(C) the shop owner can't come to the shop because of the blizzard.
(D) the customer demands the flower right away.

39.Which of the following flowers are not currently available in the flower shop?

(A) begonias
(B) lavenders
(C) carnations
(D) lilies

40.What industry does the female speaker most likely work in?

(A) flower
(B) wedding
(C) shipment
(D) design

41.How did these flowers get shipped during the storm?

(A) cut corners
(B) by a jet plane
(C) by two major transportations
(D) through relations

42.What could be the truck driver's plan on the Valentine's Day?

(A) ask the woman out on a date
(B) get the double fee for the shipment
(C) buy the flower at a discount
(D) inform the woman about a shoplifter

43.Under what circumstance, will the woman get a day off?

(A) have a huge customer for lilies
(B) a date from an admirer
(C) all merchandise is out of stock
(D) flowers miraculously arrive at the shop during the storm

44.Why does the woman say, "that makes you on top of the list"?

(A) because they are hired
(B) because she likes the guys a lot and quite suitable for the requirement
(C) because she has the authority to move them up
(D) because passion is the key

45.How did the man learn about the recruitment?

(A) pamphlets and the website
(B) the school

(C) bulletin board
(D) news report

46.Where most likely is the conversation taking place?
(A) in the campus
(B) in the interview room
(C) at the travel agency
(D) at a process plant

47.Why does the man say, "I'm counting the time"?
(A) he really wants to be on time.
(B) he cannot wait for this to be over.
(C) he knows perfectly well about the concept of time management
(D) he has a feeling that counting the time makes time pass quicker.

48.What are the speakers mainly discussing?
(A) the dishes in the lunchbox
(B) the wearisome look they are getting per day
(C) the treatment and the job content
(D) the holiday after the work

49.Where most likely is the conversation taking place?
(A) in a restaurant
(B) outside the supervisor's office
(C) in the kitchen
(D) at the factory

50.What is the request of the men?
(A) rewrite the contract
(B) renegotiate the contract
(C) demand a better offer
(D) free from the bond of the agreement

51.**Why does the boss say "we are out of workforce"?**
(A) because he wants the guys to know about his predicament
(B) to let the guys know that short-staffed problems are temporary
(C) to let the guys know that the current situation makes him hard to concede
(D) because it's not an off-season

52.**Which of the following is not what makes the two guys displeased?**
(A) what's written on the brochure
(B) what's being said during the interview
(C) what's written on websites
(D) what's being said about the barbecue

53.**What is the highest price that the woman can offer?**
(A) US 70,000
(B) US 100,000
(C) US 90,000
(D) US 200,000

54.**According to the manager, what is the regular price for the wedding?**
(A) US 70,000
(B) US 90,000
(C) US 100,000
(D) US 200,000

55.**Why does the woman say, "fritter away the money"?**
(A) she wants to profuse the money
(B) she thinks it's good for the economy and the flow of cash
(C) she thinks money can solve all problems
(D) she is mentioning that as the lifestyle of the rich

56.Why does the man come to the company?

(A) he wants to see the castle
(B) he is on behalf of the governor Clarke
(C) he is the representative here for a mission
(D) he needs hot cappuccino

57.Why does the man say, "now I have to do the heavy lifting"?

(A) he hates the heavy workload but still has to do it.
(B) he considers himself unlucky
(C) he doesn't want to be a representative
(D) he is making a complaint that he has to do his coworker's daunting job while she is on vacation

58.What is not mentioned about the third building?

(A) it contains a castle.
(B) it has an underground tunnel.
(C) there lives a real prince.
(D) there is a buffet in there.

item	remuneration
7-day Dubai trip	US 250
5-day Russia trip	US 200
14-day West Europe	US 750
14-day South Europe	US 850

59.Why is the customer calling?

(A) she wants to cancel the trip because it's not humane
(B) she thinks she has been fooled by the company
(C) she has doubts about the camel riding service
(D) she doesn't want the camel in the picture

60.Why does the customer say, "that thought does cross my mind"?

(A) she wants to be totally honest with the sales rep
(B) she finds that thought disturbing
(C) the idea of the camel riding makes her doubt about this trip
(D) she wants to keep her fingers crossed so that those camels are properly taken care of

61.Look at the graph. If the customer is cancelling the trip, what monetary reward will the sales rep lose?

(A) US 250
(B) US 200
(C) US 750
(D) US 850

62.What concern does the man mention?

(A) the watch is a second-hand
(B) the watch is a knock-off
(C) the watch does not have the waterproof function
(D) the watch is a real one

63.What must the man do?

(A) get the watch examined by a great master
(B) demand the store to reimburse him
(C) call the police
(D) inform his best friend about the watch

64.What problem has the woman identified?

(A) the counterfeit watch cannot detect water pressure
(B) the fake watch is a false alarm
(C) underwater conditions will be misjudged
(D) the man's best friend will be furious

65.Why is the man calling?

(A) to cancel the order of the long bench
(B) to inquire about the furniture that was mistakenly sent
(C) to make a purchase
(D) to give his bank account

66.What furniture is incorrectly delivered to the man's house?

(A) a short bench
(B) a bed
(C) item 65
(D) item 120

67.What is the solution offered by the woman?

(A) the man should go to the bank himself
(B) she will send the delivery guy to get the furniture
(C) she wants the man to transfer the money
(D) she demands further charges

68.Where most likely is the conversation taking place?

(A) at a bank
(B) at the police station
(C) at the headquarter
(D) at the computer lab

69.Why does the woman say, "I'm no computer prodigy"?

(A) she really wants to be humble in front of her colleague
(B) she hasn't passed the advanced computer test
(C) she is not proficient enough to maintain the operation of the system
(D) she wants to be a computer genius to take down hackers

70.Why does the man say "our computer system is encountering a bit of a snag"?

(A) he wants the lady to come tomorrow

(B) he tries to explain and makes a clarification about the delay
(C) he wants the lady to know he has no obligation to do that
(D) he wants to snag the transaction because it's illegal

模擬試題 解析

PART 3

聽力原文和對話

Questions 32-34 refer to the following conversation

Cindy: great...now I have to tell lies...and imagine how many lies I have to spin while I'm in the economy class cabin...

Jason: what do you mean...lies?

Cindy: yep...L-I-E-S...lies...whenever a customer asks me something...I have to calm he or she by saying something that is just not true...

Jason: it's just a white lie...

Cindy: ...just...we are having engine troubles...and all I can say is that's not a big deal...it can be easily fixed...don't worry about it...more wine...white or red...I knew you prefer red...red wine right away...

Jason: I'm afraid that's part of our job...

Cindy: OMG...FIRE...in the cockpit...what am I supposed to do?

Jason: put out the fire...quick...but definitely not using what's holding in your hands...

Cindy: yep...it will only make things worse.

問題32-34，請參考以下對話內容

辛蒂：好棒喔...現在我必須要說謊...試想我要編織多少的謊話，當我在經濟艙時...

傑森：對於「謊言」...你所指的是什麼呢?

辛蒂：是啊...L-I-E-S...謊言...每當有客人問我一些事情時...我必須要安撫他或她，然後要說些不是那麼真實的事情。

傑森：這只是善意的謊言...。

辛蒂：...只是...我們有引擎問題...而我所能說的是沒什麼大不了的...這很輕易就能修復...別擔心...需要更多酒嗎？...我知道你偏好紅酒...紅酒馬上到...

傑森：恐怕這就是我們工作的一部分...。

辛蒂：我的天啊！...火...在駕駛艙...我該怎麼辦?

傑森：快點...將火撲滅...但是千萬別使用你手上正拿著的東西...。

辛蒂：是呀...這只會讓事情更糟了。

試題中譯與解析

32. Where most likely is the conversation taking place? (A) in a restaurant (B) at a wine cellar (C) in the kitchen (D) **on the airplane**	32. 對話最有可能發生在何處? (A) 在餐廳 (B) 在酒窖 (C) 在廚房 (D) **在飛機上**
33. What does the man recommend? (A) take the complaint to the customer (B) tell customers the truth (C) **do as instructed** (D) give customers more expensive wine	33. 男子建議什麼呢? (A) 向顧客抱怨 (B) 告訴顧客實情 (C) **遵照指示做** (D) 給予顧客更多的紅酒

34. Why does the man say, "definitely not using what's holding in your hands"? (A) to extinguish the fire (B) **to remind the woman** (C) to control the situation (D) to cultivate the relationship	34. 為何男子提到「definitely not using what's holding on your hands」？ (A) 撲滅火源 (B) **提醒女子** (C) 控制情況 (D) 培養關係

答案：32. D 33. C 34. B

解析

- **第32題**，從對話中最一開始的在economy class cabin等訊息跟後來的在cockpit，均可以推斷對話發生的地點會是在飛機上，故要選**選項D**。
- **第33題**，男子建議的是I'm afraid that's part of our job，其實並沒有煽動或影響另名空服員，而這也是在向女空服員說道就照做吧或這是公司規定，所以要選**選項C do as instructed**。
- **第34題**，男子會說這句的原因是出於提醒，比較是幽默式的提醒對方，因為得知女空服員手上拿的是紅酒，故要選**選項B**。

聽力原文和對話

Questions 35-37 refer to the following conversation

Examiner: enter the cabin...

Cindy: OK...wow...for real...lots of smoke...that's not good

Examiner: so how are you going to respond...?

Cindy: (coughing)...wow the fire is too big...I'm kneeing down...I need some fresh air...

Examiner: 20 seconds...and still cannot do anything about it...

Cindy: what?...am I getting a bad review?...

Examiner: didn't you learn anything at the training school...?

Cindy: ...see...I'm already doing something...using both hands to clear up the fog...

Examiner: ...that's all you can do?...I guess I am going to comment...a contestant who can't seem to understand the task and probably need more time...next one

Cindy: wait a second...I just figured something out...I'm putting my clinical mask...and I lean towards the passenger seat, telling passengers...evacuate...quick...quick...

Examiner: ...game over...loose cannon...next one...

Cindy: don't you think you are overreacting...?

問題35-37，請參考以下對話內容

檢測官：進飛機客艙...
辛　蒂：好的...哇！...來真的...煙霧好大...這不太好。
檢測官：所以，你要如何反應...呢?
辛　蒂：（咳嗽）... 哇！這火太大了...我要蹲下了...我需要一些新鮮空氣...。
檢測官：20秒了...而卻完全沒轍...
辛　蒂：什麼？...我拿到負面的評論了嗎？...
檢測官：你在訓練學校的時候沒有學到任何相關的東西嗎？...
辛　蒂：...瞧...我已經正在做了...使用我的雙手揮散大霧...
檢測官：...這就是你所能做的嗎？...我想我要評論...一個受評者似乎無法了解這項任務而且可能需要更多時間...下一位。
辛　蒂：等一下...我正好想到了要怎麼做了...我戴上我的醫護面具...而且我倚身靠向乘坐椅，告訴乘客...撤離...快點...快點
檢測官：...遊戲結束了...鬆螺絲...下一位...
辛　蒂：你不覺得你有點反應過度了嗎...?

試題中譯與解析

35. What industry do the speakers most likely work in? (A) fire-fighting (B) **airline** (C) police (D) safety training	35. 說話者最有可能在哪個行業工作? (A) 消防 (B) **航空業** (C) 警局 (D) 安全訓練
36. What is the problem? (A) the smoke is too heavy. (B) using both hands to clear up the fog is not enough. (C) **the woman fails to do the task** (D) the woman shouldn't use the mask	36. 發生什麼問題? (A) 煙霧太濃厚了。 (B) 使用雙手除掉霧不太足夠。 (C) **女子執行任務失敗。** (D) 女子不應該使用面罩。

37. Why does the woman say, "don't you think you are overreacting..."? (A) she knows in advance that the examiner is going to overreact. (B) she doesn't want the examiner to act like this way. (C) she is pointing out the problem of the examiner. (D) **she is being dramatic about how the examiner said about her.**	37. 為何女子提到「don't you think you are overreacting...」？ (A) 她事先知道檢測官將會反應過度。 (B) 她不想要檢測官以這樣的方式表現。 (C) 她正指出檢測官的問題。 (D) **她只是對於檢測官講述她的評論而表現的戲劇化。**

答案：35. B 36. C 37. D

解析

- **第35題**，這題是詢問說話者所從事的產業，從對話中的enter the cabin等可以推斷說話者是航空業，很可能是測驗官在訓練中心中考空服員，故要選擇**選項B**。
- **第36題**，而主要的問題是女子無法完成任務，故要選擇**選項C**。
- **第37題**，經過對話內容後可以看出女子比較隨意、搞笑的一面，最後沒有反省自己，還反問這句真的只有dramatic可以形容了，這題最適合的選項是**選項D**。

聽力原文和對話

Questions 38-40 refer to the following conversation

Cindy: I was told by the shop owner that there is going to be a blizzard...so flowers won't be arrived until next Tuesday...

Jake: ...but it's Valentine's Day...and if you guys don't have any flowers to sell...what are you going to do...?

Cindy: ...thank god...we do have lavenders and carnations ready...in-house cultivation...in an artificial setting where temperatures are controlled...

Jake: ...what about roses...I need pink roses...a few dozens and other flowers...

Cindy: are they used for the wedding centerpiece? What about begonias? Let me show you those...strikingly beautiful...

Jake: ...wow...looks great...how much?

Cindy: ...since you are a regular...there's gonna be a discount...you know it...and what else do you need?

Jake: ...lilies...the petals will be used in the wedding main gate...

Cindy: ...I don't think that would be a problem...

問題38-40，請參考以下對話內容

辛蒂：我聽花店的老闆説即將要有一場大雪...所以花直到下周二後才會抵達。

傑克：...但是這是情人節...而且如果你們沒有花可以銷售，你們要怎麼辦?

辛蒂：...謝天謝地...我們確實備有薰衣草和康乃馨...室內耕種...在溫度受控制的人工環境裡頭。

傑克：...那麼關於玫瑰花呢？...我需要粉紅色的玫瑰花...幾打還有其他的花朵...。

辛蒂：它們是用於婚禮餐桌上的中心擺飾品嗎？那麼秋海棠呢？讓我向妳展示那些...美麗耀眼...。

傑克：...哇！...看起來很棒...多少錢?

辛蒂：...既然你是常客...會給你折扣...你知道的...你還有需要什麼嗎?

傑克：...百合...花瓣會用於婚禮的主要通道...。

辛蒂：...我不認為這會有什麼問題。

試題中譯與解析	
38. What is the problem? (A) **the shipment of the flowers will be postponed.** (B) the artificial setting for the flower is malfunctioned. (C) the shop owner can't come to the shop because of the blizzard. (D) the customer demands the flower right away.	38. 發生什麼問題? (A) **花朵的運送將會延期。** (B) 替花朵所做的人工環境故障了。 (C) 花店雇主因為暴風雪而不能來花店。 (D) 顧客要求立即拿到花朵。
39. Which of the following flowers are not currently available in the flower shop? (A) begonias (B) lavenders (C) carnations (D) **lilies**	39. 下列哪種花現在在花店中沒有存貨呢? (A) 秋海棠 (B) 薰衣草 (C) 康乃馨 (D) **百合**
40. What industry does the female speaker most likely work in? (A) **flower** (B) wedding (C) shipment (D) design	40. 女性說話者最有可能從事什麼行業呢? (A) **花朵** (B) 婚宴 (C) 運輸 (D) 設計
答案：38. A 39. D 40. A	

解析

- **第38題**，主要問題是因為有暴風雪所以花無法如期送到，所以要選**選項A**，延期。
- **第39題**，這題要注意到好幾個細節點，we do have lavenders and carnations ready和What about begonias? Let me show you those，僅能確定的是花店目前有的花有ABC三項，故答案為**選項D**。
- **第40題**，這題很明顯，女子工作的產業是花業，故要選**選項A**。

聽力原文和對話

Questions 41-43 refer to the following conversation

Cindy: ...wait a second...the truck arrived...a total life saver...
Jake: ...ok...I'm gonna wait here...
Cindy: ...I thought the weather is bad enough that flowers won't be arrived until next week...
Jason: yep...snowstorms...but those flowers are shipped through air travel and then are delivered by the vehicle...
Cindy: ...where do you need me to sign?...the same place as usual...
Jason: ...the same column...totally an unrelated topic...I guess you won't be available during the Valentine's Day..
Cindy: ...are you kidding...our busiest time..
Jason: ...ok...I get it...
Cindy: ...unless all flowers are sold out before the festival...and normally that's not gonna happen...and you have to excuse me...I have a huge customer waiting inside...
Jake: ...wow early shipment...now you are relieved...
Cindy: ...yeah...and see several boxes right over there...enough lilies for your wedding...

問題41-43，請參考以下對話內容

辛蒂：...等一下...卡車抵達了...全然是個救星...。
傑克：...好...我想在這等著...。
辛蒂：...我以為天氣遭到花朵要到下周才能抵達了...。
傑森：是的...暴風雪...但是這些花朵是透過空運，然後以陸上交通工具運送至此...。
辛蒂：...你需要我簽在哪頭呢？...一樣是在之前同樣的地方...。
傑森：...相同的欄位...全然不相干的話題...我想你在情人節期間就不會有空了...。
辛蒂：...你在開玩笑嗎？...我們最忙的時候...。
傑森：好...我知道了。
辛蒂：...除非所有的花朵都在節慶前賣光吧...通常這種事情是不可能發生的...而且請見諒一下...我有個超大個客戶在裡面等著...。
傑克：哇！提早到貨...現在你如釋重負了...。
辛蒂：...是呀...還有你看那裡那幾箱...足夠你婚禮要使用的百合花了。

試題中譯與解析	
41. How did these flowers get shipped during the storm? (A) cut corners (B) by a jet plane (C) **by two major transportations** (D) through relations	41. 在風暴期間，這些花朵是如何運送的呢? (A) 抄捷徑 (B) 藉由噴射機 (C) **藉由兩種主要的交通工具** (D) 透過關係
42. What could be the truck driver's plan on Valentine's Day? (A) **ask the woman out on a date** (B) get the double fee for the shipment (C) buy the flower at a discount (D) inform the woman about a shoplifter	42. 在情人節時，卡車司機最可能的計劃是什麼呢? (A) **約女子約會** (B) 獲取兩倍的運送費用 (C) 以折扣價格購買花朵 (D) 告知女子關於偷竊的事
43. Under what circumstance, will the woman get a day off? (A) have a huge customer for lilies (B) a date from an admirer (C) **all merchandise is out of stock** (D) flowers miraculously arrive at the shop during the storm	43. 在什麼情況下，女子將有可能獲得一天假? (A) 有個訂購百合的巨大客戶 (B) 有愛慕者的約會 (C) **所有商品都沒有存貨** (D) 在風暴期間，花朵都奇蹟似地抵達店裡頭了
答案：41. C 42. A 43. C	

解析

- **第41題**，這題可以對應到but these flowers are shipped through air travel and then are delivered by the vehicle，所以是由空運和陸運的方式，也就是答案選項表達的兩種主要交通運送方式，故答案為**選項C**。
- **第42題**，這題是考推測的部分，最有可能的是要約女子出去，所以答案為**選項A**。
- **第43題**，這題要把the woman get a day off和對話中的unless all flowers are sold out before the festival...and normally that's not gonna happen聯想起來，所以女子要在該天放假的話，等同花店的花均要銷售一空，所以要選**選項C**，all merchandise is out of stock。

聽力原文和對話

Questions 44-46 refer to the following conversation

Interviewer: what we are looking for is muscularly-built guys who can move the frozen fish in a quick manner...

Jason: I think my buddy and I will fit right in...we are junior students and would love to make some money during the vacation and I read the description from job hunt and pamphlets that there will be plenty of free time after the first few weeks of fish shipment...that's wonderful...

Interviewer: ...the heavy work takes about four, five weeks top and the rest of the time is yours...so you get to enjoy yourself during the whole trip...

Jason: ...how many vacancies are left?

Interviewer: ...two..actually...and I just love your enthusiasm...that makes you on the top of the list...

Jason: ...thanks...but when will we know the result...

Interviewer: ...normally...we don't do this....but I am telling you...you two are hired...

Jason: ...I'm so thrilled...

問題44-46，請參考以下對話內容

面試官：我們要找尋的是體格健壯的男生，能夠快速地搬動冷凍的魚...。

傑　森：我想我夥伴和我超級適合的...我們兩個是大三的學生，想要在假期期間賺取一些錢，然後我從獵人頭和小冊子那裡讀到關於這份工作，在前幾週的魚運輸後會有許多的自由時間...那樣是很棒的...。

面試官：...那樣沉重的工作大概最多只會花費4到5週而已，然後其餘的時間是你自己的...所以你在整個假期期間你也能夠自我享受的...。

傑　森：...還會有多少的空缺呢?

面試官：實際上還有...兩個...而我真的很喜愛你們的熱忱...這讓你們兩個列於清單前端了...。

傑　森：...謝謝...但是我們什麼時候能夠得知結果呢...?

面試官：...通常...我們不這樣做的...但是我現在告訴你們...你們兩個都錄取了...

傑森：...我感到很興奮...。

試題中譯與解析

44. Why does the woman say, "that makes you on top of the list"? (A) because they are hired (B) **because she likes the guys a lot and quite suitable for the requirement** (C) because she has the authority to move them up (D) because passion is the key	44. 為何女子提到「that makes you on top of the list」? (A) 因為他們被雇用了 (B) **因為她很喜歡男子而且覺得他們相當符合需求** (C) 因為她有權能把他們移到前頭 (D) 因為熱情是關鍵
45. How did the man learn about the recruitment? (A) **pamphlets and the website** (B) the school (C) bulletin board (D) news report	45. 男子是如何得知招募的? (A) **手冊和網站** (B) 學校 (C) 公佈欄 (D) 新聞報導

46. Where most likely is the conversation taking place? (A) in the campus (B) **in the interview room** (C) at the travel agency (D) at a process plant	46. 對話最有可能發生在何處呢? (A) 在校園裡頭 (B) **在面試間** (C) 在旅行社 (D) 在加工廠
答案：44. B 45. A 46. B	

- **第44題**，這題要注意的是makes you on top of the list不代表錄取了，僅代表面試官對他們印象極好、很可能錄用或對方條件很接近公司想要的，故答案要選擇**選項B**。
- **第45題**，這題很明顯是由手冊和網站上看到的，所以要選**選項A**。
- **第46題**，對話最有可能的是發生在面試房間，故答案為**選項B**。

聽力原文和對話

Questions 47-49 refer to the following conversation

Jason: it's kind of awful...living in such a filthy place...and the heavy workload...

Mike: I'm counting the time...they told us that there is going to be a few weeks that we don't have to work...right?

Jason: ...yeah...that's what they said...but I'm hoping that it's true...

Mike: ...what do you mean?

Jason: ...by the way they are treating us and other workers...I am starting to doubt about the whole deal...and we signed the contract for two months...

Mike: ...I'm so not in a mood to talk about this...I'm too exhausted...

Jason: ...it's about noon...let's go get the lunchbox...

Mike: ...today's lunchbox better be good; otherwise, I'm going to make a complaint to the supervisor here...

Jason: ...I feel so bad for dragging you into this...

問題47-49，請參考以下對話內容

傑森：有點糟糕...居住在如此骯髒的地方...還有沉重的工作負擔在...。

麥克：我在數時間了...他們告訴我會有幾週是我們不用工作的時候...對吧？

傑森：...是的...這是他們當初說的...但是我現在只希望這是真的...。

麥克：...你指的是什麼呢？

傑森：...藉由他們對待我們和其他工人們...我開始懷疑著整個交易...而我們簽了兩個月的合約...。

麥克：我真的沒心情去談這些了...我真的筋疲力盡了...。

傑森：...快到中午了...我們去拿午餐盒吧...。

麥克：...今天的午餐盒最好給我很棒，否則的話，我要向這裡的上司抱怨了...。

傑森：...把你捲進這份工作裡讓我感到很抱歉...。

試題中譯與解析

47. Why does the man say, "I'm counting the time"? (A) he really wants to be on time. (B) **he cannot wait for this to be over.** (C) he knows perfectly well about the concept of time management (D) he has a feeling that counting the time makes time pass quicker.	47. 為何男子提及「I'm counting the time」？ (A) 他真的想要準時。 (B) **他等不及要這件事情快點結束了。** (C) 他深知時間管理的概念。 (D) 他有種感覺就是數時間讓時間過得更快些。
48. What are the speakers mainly discussing? (A) the dishes in the lunchbox (B) the wearisome look they are getting per day (C) **the treatment and the job content** (D) the holiday after the work	48. 說話者們主要在討論什麼？ (A) 午餐盒內的佳餚 (B) 他們每日日益疲倦的面容 (C) **對待和工作內容** (D) 工作後的假期

49. Where most likely is the conversation taking place? (A) in a restaurant (B) outside the supervisor's office (C) in the kitchen (D) **at the factory**	49. 這段對話最有可能發生在何處? (A) 在餐廳 (B) 在管理者的辦公室外頭 (C) 在廚房 (D) **在工廠**

答案：47. B 48. C 49. D

- 第47題，男子會講這句話的主因是，他在算日子了，代表日子不好過，他只想要快點結束這件事，故答案為**選項B**。
- 第48題，有幾個選項均是對話中提到的細節點，不過最主要的原因是**選項C**，關於工作內容的不滿和對待員工的方式。
- 第49題，對話最有可能發生的地點在工廠，而對話到一半剛好快正午，他們要取拿午餐盒，所以答案要選**選項D**。

聽力原文和對話

Questions 50-52 refer to the following conversation

Jason: ...I can't stand it any longer...and we smell like dead fish...can't believe we were dumb enough to believe what's written on the brochure and what's on websites...and the HR personnel is such a liar...they are treating us like an idiot...baiting...naïvely young college students...let's go talk to the boss...

Jason: ...we'd like to release the contract...and go back to our country...

Boss: that's impossible...I need you guys here...and you agreed to be here...plus we are out of workforce here...can't you see that?...and those salmon only come in this season...if it was an off-season...I'd say yes...but now...no...and I'm begging you to stay...tonight I'm hosting a barbecue party for you guys...please stay...

Jason: fine...the party better be good...

問題50-52，請參考以下對話內容

傑森：...我無法再忍受了...然後我們聞起來像是死魚一般...無法相信我們笨到足以相信在手冊上所寫和網站上的部分...而人事專員是如此的騙子...他們把我們當成了白痴了...誘導...天真爛漫的年輕大學學生們...我們去跟老闆說吧...。

傑森：...我們想要從合約中釋放出來...然後回到我們的國家...。

老闆：這是不可能的...我需要你們在這兒...而且你們當初同意到這兒...再說，我們這裡極缺人力...你們看不到嗎？...而且那些鮭魚只有在這個季節上來...如果是淡季的話，那麼我就會答應...但是現在的話...不行...而現在我乞求你們待著...今晚我會辦個烤肉派對...請待著吧...。

傑森：好吧...那個派對最好給我很棒...。

試題中譯與解析

50. What is the request of the men? (A) rewrite the contract (B) renegotiate the contract (C) demand a better offer (D) **free from the bond of the agreement**	50. 男子的要求是什麼? (A) 重寫合約 (B) 重新協商合約 (C) 要求更佳的待遇 (D) **從合約中的束縛中解脫**
51. Why does the boss say "we are out of workforce"? (A) because he wants the guys to know about his predicament (B) to let the guys know that short-staffed problems are temporary (C) **to let the guys know that the current situation makes him hard to concede** (D) because it's not an off-season	51. 為何老闆提到「we are out of workforce」? (A) 因為他想要男子們了解他的困境。 (B) 讓男子們知道人力短缺的問題是暫時的。 (C) **讓男子們知道現在的情況讓他更難讓步。** (D) 因為這不是淡季。

52. Which of the following is not what makes the two guys displeased? (A) what's written on the brochure (B) what's being said during the interview (C) what's written on websites (D) **what's being said about the barbecue**	52. 下列哪一項不是兩位男子所不滿的部分? (A) 所寫在手冊上的內容 (B) 在面試中所提到的部分 (C) 在網站中所撰寫的部分 (D) **所提及的烤肉的部分**

答案：50. D 51. C 52. D

- **第50題**，男子所提出的要求是we'd like to release the contract，這部分對應到了free from the bond of the agreement，所以答案為**選項D**。
- **第51題**，老闆講這句話的原因可能要思考下，有幾個選項講的是事實，但不太是老闆講這句話的原因，老闆講這句話的原因其實代表了不太可能讓步，因為就沒有足夠人力了，還能讓員工解約嗎？這樣一來人手更為不足了，所以才講這句話，讓他們知難而退，故答案為**選項C**。
- **第52題**，對話中有提到幾項讓兩位男子不快的原因，但D選項很明顯不是原因，故答案為**選項D**。

聽力原文和對話

Questions 53-55 refer to the following conversation

Mary: ...you are an early bird...
Cindy: ...I guess I am...so is that a yes...
Mary: ...I don't think that would be a problem...
Cindy: ...so what's the going rate...? US 70,000?
Mary: ...you know how many celebrities want to have a wedding in our aquarium...
Cindy: ...is that within the range...I can't possibly go higher than US 100,000
Mary: ...normally...it's US 90,000 ...but still it depends...
Cindy: ...what do you mean...?
Mary: ...on how luxurious that wedding is...the senator Lincoln's wedding cost US 200,000 dollars...
Cindy: ...no way...
Mary: ...an excellent wedding band is gonna cost you extra....
Cindy: ...I guess rich people have to find a way to fritter away the money...
Mary: ...there are still too many details that we need to discuss...I just can't tell you how much a wedding is...

問題53-55，請參考以下對話內容

瑪莉：...你是個早鳥唉！...。
辛蒂：...我想我是吧...所以答案是可以囉...。
瑪莉：...我不覺得會有什麼問題...。
辛蒂：...所以價格上會是多少呢？七萬美元嗎？
瑪莉：...你知道有多少名人想要在我們水族館辦婚禮...。
辛蒂：...我提的價格在範圍之內嗎？...我無法定高於10萬美元喔。
瑪莉：...通常...價格在9萬美元...但仍然要視情況而定...。
辛蒂：...你的意思是...？
瑪莉：...要視婚宴的豪華程度而定囉...林肯議員的婚宴就花了20萬美元囉...。
辛蒂：不是吧...。
瑪莉：...一個卓越的婚宴樂隊又會花上額外的錢...。
辛蒂：我猜想有錢人必須要找個將錢揮霍掉的方式...。
瑪莉：...還有很多細節是需要討論的部分...我無法告訴你一場婚宴要花費多少囉。

試題中譯與解析	
53. What is the highest price that the woman can offer? (A) US 70,000 (B) **US 100,000** (C) US 90,000 (D) US 200,000	53. 對話中女子所能提供的最高金額為多少呢? (A) 70,000 美元 (B) **100,000 美元** (C) 90,000 美元 (D) 200,000 美元
54. According to the manager, what is the regular price for the wedding? (A) US 70,000 (B) **US 90,000** (C) US 100,000 (D) US 200,000	54. 根據經理所述，婚宴的常規價格為多少呢? (A) 70,000 美元 (B) **90,000 美元** (C) 100,000 美元 (D) 200,000 美元
55. Why does the woman say, "fritter away the money"? (A) she wants to profuse the money (B) she thinks it's good for the economy and the flow of cash (C) she thinks money can solve all problems (D) **she is mentioning that as the lifestyle of the rich**	55. 為何女子提及「fritter away the money」? (A) 她想要揮霍這筆錢。 (B) 她認為這對於經濟和現金流來說是件好事。 (C) 她認為金錢可以解決所有的問題。 (D) **她提及這是富人的生活型態。**
答案：53. B 54. B 55. D	

解析

- **第53題**，這題要對應到I can't possibly go higher than US 100,000，故答案為**選項B**。
- **第54題**，這題要對應到normally...it's US 90,000 dollars，故答案為**選項B**。
- **第55題**，主要是因為富人的生活方式才提到這點的，所以答案為**選項D**。

聽力原文和對話

Questions 56-58 refer to the following conversation

Jason: ...I'm representing ABC Drug Store for the wedding venue...

Employee: ...please...wait here...and do you need a cup of coffee...?

Jason: ...hot..cappuccino thanks

Employee: ...I will be here right away...

Mary: ...hey...I heard that Cindy is on vacation...

Jason: ...lucky for her...now I have to do the heavy lifting...

Mary: ...(chuckling)...let me show you hundreds of slides in the conference room

Jason: ...sure...

Mary: ...this one was governor Clark's wedding...romantic and luxurious...

Jason: ...I didn't know your aquarium has a castle...

Mary: ...it's somewhere near our third building...after the bride and groom walking down the tunnel in the basement... there is a huge cafeteria...an all-you-can-eat buffet...in the castle...it's like prince and princess eating in the castle...

Jason: ...I'm sure my boss is gonna love this one...but I can't make the decision for him though...

問題56-58，請參考以下對話內容

傑森：... 我是代表ABC藥品店來看婚宴的場地...。

員工：請...在這稍等...還有你真的需要一杯咖啡...。

傑森：...熱的...卡布奇諾...謝謝。

員工：我馬上就回來...。

瑪莉：...嗨...我聽說辛蒂正在放大假...。

傑森：...她走運囉...我現在要做沉重的工作...。

瑪莉：...（呵呵）...讓我在會議室向你展示數百張簡報圖。

傑森：...當然...。

瑪莉：...這是州長克拉克的婚禮...浪漫且豪華...。

傑森：...我不知道你們水族館有間城堡...?

瑪莉：...這位於接近我們第三棟建築物...在新娘和新郎走入地下室的隧道中時...有間大型的自助餐廳...吃到飽自助餐...在城堡裡頭...就像是王子和公主在城堡裡頭用餐一樣...。

傑森：...我確信我們老闆一定會很喜愛這個的...但是我不能替他做決定就是了...。

試題中譯與解析	
56. Why does the man come to the company? (A) he wants to see the castle (B) he is on behalf of the governor Clarke (C) **he is the representative here for a mission** (D) he needs hot cappuccino	56. 為什男子來公司拜訪呢? (A) 他想要觀看城堡。 (B) 他代表州長克拉克。 (C) **他身為代表來這是有任務的。** (D) 他需要熱卡布奇諾。
57. Why does the man say, "now I have to do the heavy lifting"? (A) he hates the heavy workload but still has to do it. (B) he considers himself unlucky (C) he doesn't want to be a representative (D) **he is making a complaint that he has to do his coworker's daunting job while she is on vacation**	57. 為何男子提及「now I have to do the heavy lifting」? (A) 他討厭繁重的工作負擔，但是仍舊必須做。 (B) 他認為自己並不幸運。 (C) 他不想要成為代表。 (D) **他正抱怨著，他必須要從事他同事令人感到畏懼的工作，而她卻在度假。**
58. What is not mentioned about the third building? (A) it contains a castle. (B) it has an underground tunnel. (C) **there lives a real prince.** (D) there is a buffet in there.	58. 關於第三大樓，沒有提到的部分是? (A) 它包含城堡。 (B) 它有著地下隧道。 (C) **裡頭住著一位王子。** (D) 裡頭有自助餐。
答案：56. B 57. C 58. D	

解析

- **第56題**，選項有改寫過，不過卻是男子來公司的主因，故要選擇**選項C**。
- **第57題**，男子講這句話意思是重擔卻落在他頭上，而同事卻去渡假，講這句話的主要原因是有點小抱怨或覺得不該是他責任範圍的事情但他卻要來扛，這題選**選項C**最為適切。
- **第58題**，對話中有提到城堡、新郎新娘就像王子公主般，但是沒有提到真實的王子住在該城堡裡頭，故要選**選項C**。

聽力原文和對話

Questions 59-61 refer to the following conversation

item	remuneration
7-day Dubai trip	US 250
5-day Russia trip	US 200
14-day West Europe	US 750
14-day South Europe	US 850

Cindy: ...Best Travel...how can I help you?

Customer: great to know that your company is also offering a camel riding service in a Dubai trip...but on second thought...it's kind of inhumane...I wondered how they are gonna treat those creatures...

Cindy: ...then perhaps...you shouldn't go...are you considering cancelling the trip?

Customer: ...that thought does cross my mind....perhaps I will just take a few pictures with the animal...and decide not to go for camel ride...

Cindy: ...it's entirely up to you

Customer: ...you have been really helpful...you are so kind...

Cindy: ...I know this is not the right place to vent...I'm feeling low today...

Customer: ...are you OK?...I'm not cancelling...so you don't have to worry about it ok...take care...

問題59-61，請參考以下對話內容

項目	報酬
7日 杜拜之旅	250 美元
5日 俄羅斯之旅	200 美元
14日 西歐之旅	750 美元
14日 南歐之旅	850 美元

辛蒂：...倍斯特旅遊...我能幫你什麼嗎?

顧客：很高興得知你們公司在杜拜旅遊時也提供一項駱駝騎乘服務...但是幾經思考後...這有點太不人道了...我在想他們會怎樣對待那些生物呢...。

辛蒂：...那麼或許...你不該前往...你正取消這項旅程嗎?

顧客：...這個想法真的在我心中浮現過...或許我就拍攝幾張跟動物的合照...然後確定不騎乘牠們...。

辛蒂：...這就要看你自己本身了...。

顧客：...你真的幫助很大...你太好了...。

辛蒂：...我知道這不是宣洩情緒的地方...但是我今天真的感到很低潮...。

顧客：...你還好嗎？...我沒有打算取消行程...所以你別擔心了...照顧好自己。

試題中譯與解析

59. Why is the customer calling?
(A) she wants to cancel the trip because it's humane
(B) she thinks she has been fooled by the company
(C) **she has doubts about the camel riding service**
(D) she doesn't want the camel in the picture

59. Why is the customer calling?
(A) 她想要取消旅程，因為這是人道的
(B) 她認為他被公司騙了
(C) **她對於駱駝騎乘的部分感到疑惑**
(D) 她不想要照片中有駱駝

60. Why does the customer say, "that thought does cross my mind"? (A) she wants to be totally honest with the sales rep (B) she finds that thought disturbing (C) **the idea of the camel riding makes her doubt about this trip** (D) she wants to keep her fingers crossed so that those camels are properly taken care of	60. 為何顧客要提及, "that thought does cross my mind"? (A) 她想要對銷售業務完全坦承 (B) 她發現那個想法干擾人心 (C) **駱駝騎乘的想法讓她對於這次的旅遊感到疑惑** (D) 她想要駱駝如願地受到完善的照顧
61. Look at the graph. If the customer is cancelling the trip, what monetary reward will the sales rep lose? (A) **US 250** (B) US 200 (C) US 750 (D) US 850	61. 請參考表格。如果顧客取消這次旅程，銷售業務會失去多少金錢獎勵？ (A) **250 美元** (B) 200 美元 (C) 750 美元 (D) 850 美元

答案：59. C 60. C 61. A

解析

- **第59題**，對話前面有提到打電話的女子其實是對於騎乘駱駝感到有疑慮，故答案為**選項C**。
- **第60題**，顧客腦海中有浮現出該想法，而講這句話的原因是因為騎乘駱駝讓她對於這次旅行產生質疑，故答案為**選項C**，其他選項都有部分切中，但不是她講這句話的原因。
- **第61題**，這題的話monetary reward對應到圖表中的remuneration，所以在杜拜的地方找到對應的金額是250美元，故答案為**選項A**。

聽力原文和對話

Questions 62-64 refer to the following conversation

Cindy: oh my god...that's a knock-off...
Jason: how do you know?
Cindy: I've been in Best Watch for twenty years...of course I can tell it's a counterfeit...
Jason: ...what should I do? I already sent it to a good friend of mine...and he is probably now diving in New Zealand...I hope he does not wear the fake one...
Cindy: good news is that the waterproof function of the fake watch is the same as that of the authentic one...
Jason: ...thanks...that's a relief...
Cindy: ...but there is bad news....
Jason: ...what...the...shoot...
Cindy: ...if you go down further than twenty feet...it will go malfunctioned...that means you can't tell the real water pressure...
Jason: ...he will definitely go ballistic if he finds out...

問題62-64，請參考以下對話內容

辛蒂：我的天啊！...那是仿冒品...。
傑森：你如何得知的呢?
辛蒂：我已經在倍斯特手錶待了20年了...當然我能分辨出這是不是仿冒品...。
傑森：...我該怎麼做呢？我已經送了一支錶給我一位好友了...而他可能現在正在紐西蘭潛水...希望他不要戴膺品...。
辛蒂：好消息是仿冒的手錶的防水功能和真品的防水功能是一樣的...。
傑森：...謝謝...真令人鬆了一口氣...。
辛蒂：...但是也有壞消息...。
傑森：...什麼...快説吧...。
辛蒂：...如果你下水超過20尺...手錶會發生故障...這意味著你無法分辨真實的水壓...。
傑森：如果他發現的話，他一定會大發雷霆...。

試題中譯與解析	
62. What concern does the man mention? (A) the watch is a second-hand (B) **the watch is a knock-off** (C) the watch does not have the waterproof function (D) the watch is a real one	62. 男子所提到的擔憂是什麼? (A) 手錶是二手品 (B) **那隻手錶是仿冒品** (C) 那隻手錶沒有防水的功能 (D) 那隻手錶是真品
63. What must the man do? (A) get the watch examined by a great master (B) demand the store to reimburse him (C) call the police (D) **inform his best friend about the watch**	63. 男子必須做什麼? (A) 去拿由大師檢查過的手錶 (B) 要求店家補償他 (C) 打電話給警方 (D) **告知他最好的朋友關於手錶的事情**
64. What problem has the woman identified? (A) the counterfeit watch cannot detect water pressure (B) the fake watch is a false alarm (C) **underwater conditions will be misjudged** (D) the man's best friend will be furious	64. 女子察覺出什麼問題? (A) 手錶贗品無法檢測出水壓 (B) 手錶仿冒品是虛驚一場 (C) **水下的情況被誤判了** (D) 男子的最好的朋友將會感到憤怒
答案：62. B 63. D 64. C	

解析

- **第62題**，男子所提到的部分是手錶是仿冒的，而這也是他所擔心的部分，故答案為**選項B**。
- **第63題**，這題是問男子必須做什麼呢，其實最主要的就是要通知他好友關於手錶的事情，故答案為**選項D**。
- **第64題**，女子所辨識到的問題有幾個，其中一項是關於手錶的防水功能，另一個是用於檢測水壓的部分，if you go down further than twenty feet...it will go malfunctioned...that means you can't tell the real water pressure...，試題選項中並未提及水壓或故障，但是卻以濃縮式的表達出該句句意，改寫成較隱晦的答案**underwater conditions will be misjudged**，故答案要選擇**選項C**。

聽力原文和對話

Questions 65-67 refer to the following conversation

Cindy: ... Best furniture...how can I help you...?
Mark: ...I didn't order the furniture that you sent to me...
Cindy: ...let me check on the computer...what is your social security number?
Mark: ...555-777-999
Cindy: ...and the date of your purchase...?
Mark: ...2025 June 8
Cindy: ...ok...let's verify....you did order item number 5, 65, 90, and 120...is that correct...?
Mark: ...yes...wait a second...I forgot that I didn't cancel item 120 in the shopping chart...it's a long bench...isn't it?
Cindy: ...yes...
Mark: ...what should I do now?
Cindy: ...let me think...our shipping guy happens to be in your area...is it ok that he goes over now and retrieves the bench...
Mark: ...sure...but how about the money...?
Cindy: ...give me your bank account...and I'm going to transfer the money to you...

問題65-67，請參考以下對話內容

辛蒂：...倍斯特傢俱...我該怎樣幫助你呢?
馬克：...我沒有訂購貴公司所寄的傢俱...。
辛蒂：...讓我在電腦上檢查一下...你的社會安全碼是多少呢?
馬克：...555-777-999。
辛蒂：...你的訂購日期是幾號?
馬克：...2025年6月8日。
辛蒂：...好的...讓我們來確認下...你曾經訂購項目5, 65, 90和120...項目正確嗎...?
馬克：...是的...等一下...我忘記了我在購物車中，沒有取消項目120...是長板凳...對吧?
辛蒂：...是的...。
馬克：我現在應該要怎麼做呢?
辛蒂：...讓我想下...我們的運送員碰巧在你住的地區...如果他現在過去那裡並且取回板凳的話，這樣ok嗎...?
馬克：...當然...但是那麼錢呢...?
辛蒂：...給我你的銀行帳號...我會將錢轉給你的...。

試題中譯與解析

65. Why is the man calling? (A) to cancel the order of the long bench (B) **to inquire about the furniture that was mistakenly sent** (C) to make a purchase (D) to give his bank account	65. 為什麼男子打此通電話? (A) 取消長板凳的訂單 (B) **詢問關於誤送的傢俱** (C) 下單訂購 (D) 交付他銀行帳戶
66. What furniture is incorrectly delivered to the man's house? (A) a short bench (B) a bed (C) item 65 (D) **item 120**	66. 什麼傢俱誤送到男子家? (A) 一張短的板凳 (B) 一張床 (C) 項目65號 (D) **項目120號**

67. What is the solution offered by the woman? (A) the man should go to the bank himself (B) **she will send the delivery guy to get the furniture** (C) she wants the man to transfer the money (D) she demands further charges	67. 對話中女子所提供的解決方法是什麼? (A) 男子應該要自行跑銀行一趟 (B) **她會派運送員去取傢俱。** (C) 她想要男子將金錢轉帳。 (D) 她索求更多的費用

答案：65. B 66. D 67. B

解析

- **第65題**，男子打電話的原因是詢問誤送的家俱，故答案要選**選項B**。
- **第66題**，誤送的家俱在對話中有提到，所以要選item 120，故答案為**選項D**。
- **第67題**，由女子所提供的辦法，也可以由對話中輕易找到，她會派人去取，故答案要選**選項B**。

聽力原文和對話

Questions 68-70 refer to the following conversation

Cindy: there is an irregular activity happening in the computer...I'm gonna shut it down for a while...

Jason: that's odd...it's gonna affect several transactions...

Cindy: that's why I'm doing the right thing...shutting it down...

Jason: hope it's not some hackers...breaking into the system...

Cindy: ...I hope not...I'm no computer prodigy...I cannot deal with hackers...and if there is a safety concern...I'm calling the headquarters and the police...

Customer: ...I wanna transfer the money...and this is the transferring form and the money...

Jason: ...may I see your ID...don't mean to trouble you...but if the transferring money exceeds to that amount...it's our obligation to see the ID...

Customer: ...here is my ID...thanks...

Jason: ...but you have to wait for a few seconds because our computer system is encountering a bit of a snag...

問題68-70，請參考以下對話內容

辛蒂：在電腦中...有著不尋常的活動...我要先將電腦關閉一陣子...。

傑森：那樣好奇怪...這會影響幾筆交易...。

辛蒂：這就是為什麼我要做對的事情...將電腦關閉...。

傑森：希望此舉不是一些駭客...入侵系統...。

辛蒂：我希望不是...我不是電腦天才...我不會跟駭客應對...而且如果有安全性的疑慮的話...我會致電給總部並且報警...。

顧客：...我想要將錢轉帳...這是轉移清單和金錢...。

傑森：...我可以看下你的ID嗎...這不意謂著麻煩到你...但是如果轉移金錢超過某個金額時...我們是有義務要看下ID的...。

顧客：...這是我的ID...謝謝。

傑森：...但是你必須要等幾秒鐘，因為電腦正遭遇到一點障礙...。

試題中譯與解析	
68. Where most likely is the conversation taking place? (A) **at a bank** (B) at the police station (C) at the headquarter (D) at the computer lab	68. 此對話最有可能發生在何處? (A) **在銀行** (B) 在警局 (C) 在總部 (D) 在電腦實驗室
69. Why does the woman say, "I'm no computer prodigy"? (A) she really wants to be humble in front of her colleague (B) she hasn't passed the advanced computer test (C) **she is not proficient enough to maintain the operation of the system** (D) she wants to be a computer genius to take down hackers	69. 為何女子提及「I'm no computer prodigy」? (A) 她真的想要在她同事面前保持謙遜。 (B) 她並未考過電腦高級考試。 (C) **她的電腦能力並未精通到足以維持電腦系統的運作。** (D) 她想要成為電腦天才以擊倒電腦駭客們。
70. Why does the man say "our computer system is encountering a bit of a snag"? (A) he wants the lady to come tomorrow. (B) **he tries to explain and makes a clarification about the delay.** (C) he wants the lady to know he has no obligation to do that. (D) he wants to snag the transaction because it's illegal.	70. 為何男子提及「our computer system is encountering a bit of a snag」? (A) 他想要女士明天再來。 (B) **他試圖解釋且澄清關於延遲的事情。** (C) 他要該女士了解，他並沒有義務要做那些事情。 (D) 他想要阻撓交易，因為其是違法的。
答案：68. A 69. C 70. B	

解析

- **第68題**，對話中有提到交易和關閉系統等等的，所以答案要選擇銀行，答案為**選項A**。
- **第69題**，女子講這句話的原因是，她並不是電腦天才，所以她也無能去維護這件事，如果銀行系統真的被入侵的話，故答案要選擇**選項C**。
- **第70題**，男子説這句話的原因是，他試圖要説明會有些許延誤的原因，故答案要選**選項B**。

國家圖書館出版品預行編目(CIP)資料

新制多益聽力題庫：會話大全 / Amanda Chou著. -- 初版. --新北市：倍斯特, 2020.09
面； 公分. -- (考用英語系列 ; 026)
ISBN 978-986-98079-6-8
（第1冊：平裝附光碟片)
1.多益測驗

805.1895 109012070

考用英語系列 026

新制多益聽力題庫：會話大全1（附MP3）

初　　版　2020年9月
定　　價　新台幣420元

作　　者　Amanda Chou
出　　版　倍斯特出版事業有限公司
發 行 人　周瑞德
電　　話　886-2-8245-6905
傳　　真　886-2-2245-6398
地　　址　23558 新北市中和區立業路83巷7號4樓
E-mail　best.books.service@gmail.com
官　　網　www.bestbookstw.com
特約編輯　陳韋佑
封面構成　高鍾琪
內頁構成　菩薩蠻數位文化有限公司
印　　製　大亞彩色印刷製版股份有限公司

港澳地區總經銷　泛華發行代理有限公司
地　　址　香港新界將軍澳工業邨駿昌街7號2樓
電　　話　852-2798-2323
傳　　真　852-3181-3973